Illusions Unveiled

Ardor Creek, Book 2

By

AYLA ASHER

Contents

*For everyone who might need just **one** more chance...*

Chapter 1

♥

P eter Stratford observed the stunning woman throw her head back and laugh at something Scott Grillo said. His buddy was quite serious and not at all witty enough to elicit such a visceral reaction, and Peter felt himself scowl. When was the last time Carrie had laughed like that with him? Searching his memory, he realized it was most likely decades ago. Although he and Carrie had repaired their relationship immensely, past hurts and mistakes would always linger between them.

That was to be expected between two people as connected and entwined as Peter and Carrie Longwood—the only woman he'd ever loved and the one he'd hurt so vehemently.

Features softening, he recalled the first time he'd ever spoken to her. One look into those sparkling green eyes and he'd given his seven-year-old heart to her, never to reclaim it again.

"Are you hurt?" a soft voice asked.

Squinting into the sun, he saw the girl's silhouette. "No."

Kneeling, she lifted her hand, gently stroking his rapidly swelling neck. "Jonathan threw the ball really hard. It was mean."

"I hate dodgeball," Peter said, kicking the dirt with his sneaker. "I wish Ms. Jones wouldn't make us play."

"I hate it too." Her button nose wrinkled, the skin pale under a smattering of freckles.

"You should probably go before Ms. Jones sees us. I always hide here but she eventually finds me. You'll get in trouble."

"I don't mind," she said, relaxing into a cross-legged position. "Daddy always says we have to look out for our neighbors. It's what Jesus wants."

"My dad says Jesus isn't real," Peter muttered. He'd never really talked to Carrie Longwood but knew she was the preacher's daughter. In their small town of Ardor Creek, Pennsylvania, everyone knew Pastor Longwood.

"I think things are real in your heart sometimes, even if you can't touch them."

"Maybe." Shrugging, he trailed a stick through the dirt. Glancing up, he asked, "Why did you follow me here?"

Her eyes were clear as she studied him. "You seemed sad."

Lowering his gaze, Peter nodded. He'd been sad a lot lately. His dad always drank a lot of beer when he came home from work, and yelled at his mom almost every night. It frightened Peter, which led to him withdrawing at school. He didn't have a lot of friends but that didn't really bother him. For some reason, Carrie was being nice and he decided to return the sentiment.

"I was sad until you came over."

Pink lips formed a sweet smile and Peter's heart clanked in his chest. It was a profound moment he'd always remember, for it was the moment he began the slide into deep, abiding love for Carrie Longwood.

"Whatcha daydreaming about over here?" the object of his musings asked, a grin on her gorgeous face.

"Just lost in memories," he said, sliding his arm across her shoulders. Holding her was as natural to him as breathing. "Did you like the ribs?"

"The new sauce was amazing. The first spring barbeque is definitely a success."

"I like having everyone over and it's been pretty warm for April. Glad you liked the brine." Squeezing her, he released, mourning the loss of her lithe body against his.

"Mom, can we go Ashlyn's and Scott's and see the new chair they got for Sally Pickens?"

Brushing her son's hair off his forehead, she nodded. "We can stop by on the way home but I don't think it's new. I think Scott just painted it a different color."

"Yep," Scott said, walking over with Carrie's younger son slung over his shoulder. "The old paint was chipping so we figured we'd give Sally an upgrade." Setting Charlie on the ground, he ruffled his hair. "You're getting really good at soccer, buddy. Nice job."

"I'm still better," Sebastian said, his lips forming a pout.

"You're both excellent," Carrie said, her tone stern but caring. She was a wonderful mother and Peter was so happy she had the boys. Carrie had wanted kids as long as he could remember and it was one of the many reasons he'd pushed her away.

In his youth, his greatest desire had been to escape Ardor Creek, with its unexciting small-town pace, and make it in the big city. Having a wife and kids was never a part of that package. Knowing Carrie craved them, he'd been cruel in an effort to push her away, hoping she would find another man to give her kids. Unfortunately, her ex-husband was an asshole of epic proportions, causing Peter to wish he hadn't made those terrible decisions. But the past had been written, no matter how fervently he longed to change it.

"You want to come?" Carrie asked, auburn eyebrows lifted.

"To see a chair? Uh, I think I'm good."

Breathing a laugh, she shrugged. "Your loss. If Sally haunts you at night just remember you didn't respect the awesomeness of her chair."

"I'm terrified." Giving a playful eye roll, he noticed her cheeks redden. Carrie always looked so pretty when she blushed, which was quite often, and it always sent a deep rush of desire through his veins. "But we're on for karaoke on Wednesday, right?"

"Sure are. I'll be heading back from Sebastian's appointment in Scranton so I might be a few minutes late. Kara is watching Charlie so the babysitting detail is already set."

"Is Sebastian still having the headaches and stomach cramps?"

"Yes," she said, glancing at her son as concern laced her features. "Dr. Stevens is a specialist and a board-certified surgeon so I hope he can help diagnose what's going on. It's so scary, Peter. When he looks at me and asks why it hurts, my heart just breaks."

"I know, honey," he said, clenching her hand. "You'll get it figured out. I can always watch Charlie too if you need me. You know you can ask me for help."

"I know," she said, squeezing back before disengaging. "Okay, let me get these rug rats on the road. Can't wait for Wednesday." She waggled her fingers before trailing off and rounding up the boys, loading them in her SUV before following Scott and Ashlyn's car down the driveway.

"Let me help you clean up, buddy," Chad Hanson said, patting his shoulder.

"It's pretty much done but you can help me take the desserts inside. Thanks, man." They were both Ardor Creek locals and had known each other since childhood. Chad was now the mayor and one of Peter's good friends. After packing up the remnants of the barbeque, they settled onto Peter's couch for one last beer as they watched the game. When Chad left, Peter took stock of the silence. His mother had passed away in January, leaving him with no remaining family and a cold, empty house. Sighing at the emptiness that encompassed his life, he prepped for bed and pulled out his journal, determined to focus on the positives.

During his last stint in rehab, Peter's therapist suggested he begin journaling. Although he thought it somewhat ridiculous and a bit new-agey for his tastes, he was determined not to hit rock bottom again and was open to trying new things. The journal was now filled with goals, intentions, musings, and statements of gratitude. It was a reminder that even though he'd squandered so much, there were still remnants of goodness in his life.

Flipping through the journal, he noted how frequently Carrie's name appeared. The entire notebook was basically a love letter to her, detailing how thankful he was for her friendship and forgiveness. In another life, he would ask her for one more chance. One more attempt to love her in all the ways she deserved and ensure he didn't blow it.

But this was reality and he was stuck in this lifetime, where he'd made so many mistakes and devolved into a junkie and degenerate. Although he was sober now, there was always the chance he'd fall off the cliff again, and he often wondered if it was fair to saddle

Carrie with that baggage. Would it even be possible for him to be a proper role model for the two boys she loved so dearly?

Peter had no idea and, therefore, he lived with his abiding love for her and hadn't pursued another chance. And if she fell in love with someone else? Peter figured he could clutch the pieces of his shattered heart and be content she was with someone whole. Imagining her happy brought him a small sliver of peace, even though the thought of her being with anyone else devastated his darkened soul.

Chapter 2

C arrie Longwood glanced at her ten-year-old son, fingers furiously moving over the hand-held video game player as he sat in the passenger seat. Thankful Sebastian was focused on the game, she let the worry surface. The weight was crushing and she struggled not to choke on her fear.

Dr. Stevens had confirmed what she'd known deep inside: her little boy was very sick. His symptoms had appeared months ago, mild and almost overlooked by Carrie, who was the polar opposite of a hypochondriac. She firmly believed most maladies could be cured with some ibuprofen and a good yoga session, and trained her boys to be tough as well.

But Sebastian had continued to complain about headaches and stomach cramps. Usually the first to rise at the crack of dawn, he'd become lethargic and tough to extricate from bed each morning. Eventually, he'd called her to the bathroom and shown her the slightly reddened trail left behind after he'd used the toilet, and Carrie's heart had leaped into her throat.

"Did it come out that color, sweetie?" she asked, kneeling and squeezing his upper arms.

Nodding, his cheeks flushed with embarrassment and Carrie ached to soothe him. Pulling him into her embrace, she felt like the absolute worst mother in the world. Her baby was sick and she'd dismissed his symptoms as normal maladies.

Springing into action, she'd taken him to the local pediatrician who'd insisted she make an appointment with the specialist in Scranton immediately. Now, returning home from that appointment, Carrie felt her world crashing down. Her mother had passed two years ago from kidney disease related to her diabetes and she feared Sebastian would inherit the disease.

"Yes!" he cried, shaking his fist in the air. "I beat Level 37, Mom!"

"That's awesome, sweetie," she said, running her hand over his dirty blond hair. He hadn't inherited her natural red color nor did he have brown hair like Charlie. Her ex-husband, Jeff, had brown hair and Charlie favored him much more than Sebastian. Of course, there were reasons for this. Reasons only Carrie knew and that had been secretly locked away for so long.

"I was going to go to the pub tonight but I think we should all hang and eat spaghetti since it's your favorite."

"Okay," he said, shrugging. "I'm starving so I might have two helpings."

"I'll make enough for us to have as many helping as we want." Focusing on the road, she tried to calm the fears. Anxiety would get her nowhere and she needed to be strong for the children she adored. Dr. Stevens had run a plethora of tests and would call her with the results on Friday. All she could do was wait.

Once home, she paid Kara and informed her she wouldn't need her for the rest of the evening. The kind high school student who lived beside her offered to come back later if she reconsidered. While the boys watched TV in the living room, Carrie prepped dinner and called Peter.

"Hey. We still on for karaoke?"

"I can't tonight," she said into the Bluetooth headset she'd placed on her ear. "The appointment was intense and I just want to hang with the boys."

"Was it bad news, honey?"

"Not yet but I'm terrified it's coming. Dr. Stevens is going to call me with the results on Friday."

"I can come over on Friday after my last appointment at four o'clock. I haven't had a pizza night with you and the boys in a while. I'd really like to be there for you after you hear the news, Carrie."

Pursing her lips, she contemplated. If only he'd made that offer during one of the moments she'd so desperately craved it over their long, hurtful past. So many times, she'd yearned for his support and comfort, only to be tossed aside. She'd always represented Ardor Creek to him and, therefore, she represented confinement. His tether to the small-town life he hated and was desperate to escape. She'd been collateral damage from his desire to flee, and it had destroyed their relationship.

When he'd returned three years ago, broken and battered by addiction and failure, he'd come to her after his month-long rehab. He'd looked her in the eye and apologized, as addicts are taught in recovery therapy, and asked for her forgiveness. The lingering anger had almost precluded her from bestowing it upon him. Only one thing spurred her decision to embrace their friendship and start again. One harrowing secret she'd kept from everyone that proved she was also capable of grave mistakes.

"Care Bear?" he asked, concerned. "You there?"

He'd called her that since they were ten after she'd developed an obsession with the silly cartoon bears. It was probably ridiculous he still used the nickname, but she cherished it as a reminder they'd once loved each other, all those years ago before they chose to throw it away. Saddened at the loss of what they could've created, she sighed. "I'm here."

"So, are you in? Pizza and pinot noir? I'll bring both. I can be there by five on Friday."

"Okay. Remember Charlie likes sausage instead of pepperoni."

"I'll get one of both. And I'll grab a nice bottle for you. I miss good wine and need to live vicariously through you. You can be my taster."

"I'm so proud of your sobriety, Peter. How many days now?"

"One thousand and thirty-one. Almost three years."

"That's amazing."

"What would be amazing is if I'd never gotten hooked on booze and drugs in the first place. I let go of being embarrassed a long time ago but the locals gave me a shit ton of side-eye. You never judged me, Carrie, even though I deserved it. I appreciate you so much."

Closing her eyes, the intense feelings pulsed deep within. She'd always loved Peter with her entire soul, even when he'd disparaged and rejected it. The emotion was a constant of which she would never be free. Carrie had accepted this ages ago and had learned to live in quiet acceptance of her never-ending feelings for the man who couldn't find it in his heart to choose her. Now that she had the boys and the baggage of a messy divorce, and he had the ghosts of his past, she understood the path to acting upon their love was closed.

Every so often, she would see a sliver of emotion in his deep blue eyes. He would gaze at her with longing as regret and sentiment swam in the orbs. But as quickly as it appeared, he would douse it, reminding Carrie she'd never been part of his plan. Peter had longed to escape Ardor Creek and conquer the world his entire life. A small-town girl with dreams of a simple family life had never fit into his well-curated plan.

"Judgement is a wasted sentiment. Throwing stones through glass houses and all."

"Is that a direct quote from Pastor Longwood?" he teased.

"Dad was a bit more eloquent than that."

"His sermons certainly held everyone's attention."

"Except yours. I think you spent most of them trying to work your hand under my Sunday dress."

Chuckling, his sexy tone made her shiver. "I still see those pretty legs in my dreams. Although that's probably creepy since we were sixteen."

"Yeah, maybe don't mention that to anyone but me. I'll let it slide. You always were pretty good with your hands."

"They had a mind of their own around you, honey."

As much as she loved flirting with him, Carrie hated wasting time on pointless things. Since she was sure she'd never feel those strong hands caress her skin again, she moved on. "Okay, we'll see you on Friday. Thanks, Peter."

"See you then."

Clicking off her headset, she sighed, stirring the large vat of sauce as Charlie ran into the kitchen. "Is it ready, Mom? I'm staaaaaaarving."

"Okay, drama king, it's ready. Set the table with your brother and you can each have one glass of soda."

As her kids torpedoed around the kitchen, she set the pasta and sauce on the table along with the garlic bread she'd toasted. Sitting down with her two greatest loves, she reveled in the sloppy spaghetti-stained smiles of her beloved boys.

Chapter 3

Peter stopped by Ardor Creek Pizza House on Friday afternoon to pick up the two pizzas. Armed with both extra-larges, he drove to Carrie's house. He figured it wouldn't hurt if they had leftovers so Carrie could get a break from cooking. She was understandably stressed about Sebastian's health situation and he wanted to help in any way he could.

Parking in her driveway, he ambled up the stairs and knocked on the door. Turning the knob, he pushed it slightly open. "Carrie? Boys? You guys home?"

"We're playing Avengers in here, Uncle Peter!" Sebastian called. Stepping inside, Peter noticed the boys plopped in front of the TV as their fingers skated over the controllers.

"Cool," he said, closing the door behind him. "Who's winning?"

"We don't really play to see who wins," Charlie said, eyes glued to the screen. "We just want to beat the levels."

"Got it," he said, walking into the kitchen and placing the pizzas on the table. "Where's your mom?"

"I'm here," Carrie said softly.

Turning, he saw her, dressed in a soft green sweater, a few shades darker than her eyes, and tight blue jeans. She looked young, so much like the teenage girl he'd lusted after once hormones invaded his body and never looked back. Noticing her red-rimmed eyes, he strode toward her.

"Bad news?" he whispered.

Nodding, she glanced toward the living room.

"Let's go on the porch. They're deep into the video game any-way."

Taking his offered hand, she clutched tightly, relaying her fear. Dying to comfort her, he threaded their fingers and led her onto the front porch.

"Uncle Peter and I will be right outside, guys," she said to the boys.

They both gave a dismissive, "Okay," and she closed the door behind her.

"Carrie," he said, tugging her toward the railing. "Tell me."

Burying her face in her hands, her shoulders shook as she began to cry. Aching for her, he pulled her into his arms. "It's okay, hon. Whatever it is, we'll make it okay. I promise."

Lifting her head, she gazed at him with wet eyes. "You can't promise that, Peter. No one can. I'm so afraid to lose him. He's my baby. I have to protect him."

"I know, honey," he said, cupping her face and swiping the tears with his thumbs. "We'll protect him together. What's the diagno-sis?"

"Both of his kidneys are failing. He most likely inherited it from my mom. One is worse than the other and is in complete failure."

"What does that mean?"

"He needs a transplant, Peter. Oh my god." Lowering her fore-head to his chest, she clutched his shirt as she cried.

"Then we'll get him a kidney, Carrie," he said, stroking her hair. "Kidney transplants are done all the time and they're relatively safe from what I've heard. It's not the end of the world. We'll find a way."

"I'm a terrible mother," she said, wiping her nose on his polo shirt. He would've been pissed if it were anyone else but Carrie had cried on his shoulder so many times, he was used to her habits. "He complained of symptoms for months and I dismissed them. I was so consumed with getting Jeff out of our lives and moving on as if everything was normal. I should be shot for how terribly I handled this."

"Carrie," he said, lifting her chin with his fingers. "I'm not the person you want to do this with. I've known you your whole damn life and there's no way in hell you're going to convince me you're not the most loving person on the planet. With those two boys?" He gestured with his head toward the house. "You're a fucking rock star. You always put them first and they're so lucky to have you. I need you to stop talking this way right now. Do you hear me?"

"Stop yelling at me," she teased, breathing a laugh as she wiped her nose.

Smiling, he tucked her hair behind her ear. "I'll yell all day until you stop beating yourself up."

Exhaling, she nodded. "Fine. It won't help anyway. Now I have to figure out what to do. Obviously, I'm going to see if I can donate one of my kidneys. I'm going to a diagnostic center tomorrow to get some tests. I need to see if my blood type matches Sebastian's. I can't believe I have no idea what my blood type is. Do you know yours?"

"No idea, actually. I should probably know that."

"Me too," she said, shrugging. "I just never had a reason to, I guess."

"I understand you wanting to donate a kidney but isn't there a donor list he can get on?"

"The wait is months to years, which would put him on dialysis and make his life full of hospital visits, tubes, and infusions. I won't put him through that if I can prevent it."

"I understand."

Sighing, she drew away and placed her hands on the rail, absently staring over the lawn. "They're all I have, Peter. Now that Mom's gone...I can't lose him."

"I would argue that you have tons of people who love you, Carrie. Scott, Ashlyn, Chad, and I are just the beginning. Everyone in Ardor Creek adores you and we'll all do whatever we can to support you. We can set up a Go Fund Me and do some fundraisers—"

"I don't want to go there yet," she said, interrupting him. "I appreciate the sentiment but, first, I just need to find an answer. Once I figure out the plan, we can worry about the costs and recovery and whatever the hell else this will require. But, for now, I need to figure out the plan. Dr. Stevens said he'll need to go on dialysis in a few weeks if he doesn't find a donor."

"Carrie," Peter breathed, sliding his arm over her shoulders and pulling her into his side. "I'm so damn sorry, honey." Placing a soft kiss on her temple, he felt her tense.

"Okay," she said, pulling away. "Enough of the pity party. I'm determined to be strong for them and the pizza's getting cold. Let's eat, and I could also really use a glass of the wine you brought."

Lips firm, he nodded, tamping down his frustration at the fact she pulled away. But Carrie often shied away from his touch since he moved back to town and he shouldn't be surprised. There were times in their lives when she'd welcomed his kisses and embraces and he'd squandered each and every one. She was like a battle-worn soldier who'd figured out that fighting losing skirmishes was futile. Hating he'd lost the ability to hold her for longer than the scant moments she allowed, he straightened.

"I got extra-larges so you'd have some leftovers."

Arching a brow, she said, "With those two heathens? I'm not sure that's possible."

Chuckling, he gestured toward the door. "Let's find out."

Following her inside, he settled into yet another night with Carrie and her boys. For someone who'd always disparaged the idea of settling down, Peter certainly enjoyed these treasured nights. If he was honest, he cherished them above all the fancy parties and expensive yacht excursions he'd had in his storied past. At the time, they'd seemed so exclusive, when his nose was full of cocaine and his liver full of tequila. Now, he understood they were all wasted moments that represented the emptiness he felt inside.

Hanging with Carrie and the kids made him feel whole. Comfortable. Stable. It was something he thought he'd never want and, now, he feared it was something he'd never deserve. In the unfairness of life, he'd hit the woeful jackpot. Still, he could enjoy the scraps he got from the close-knit family and bask in the moments they shared with him. Vowing to do just that, he grabbed a plate from the paper stack Carrie threw on the coffee table and took a huge bite of the sausage pizza, happy it was Charlie's favorite since it was his favorite too.

Chapter 4

♥

Carrie's phone rang on Monday afternoon as she sat at her desk at Grillo Design and Construction. Noting Dr. Stevens' office number on the caller ID, she stepped outside onto the sidewalk, thankful it wasn't swarmed with people. Lifting the phone to her ear, she noticed her shaking hand.

"Hello?"

"Carrie, it's Dr. Stevens. Is this a good time?"

"Yes. Did you look over the blood test results I emailed over?"

"Yes. Unfortunately, you and Sebastian are not a match."

"Oh, I assumed he had Type A blood as well."

"Sebastian has Type O blood which was inherited from his father since you're Type A. Type O blood requires a kidney transplant from an O donor. Unfortunately, you're not a candidate to donate a kidney."

Carrie closed her eyes as dread coursed through her body. The weight of the repercussions of the news was vast.

"I know this wasn't the news you were looking for, and I'm very sorry to have to deliver it, but you honestly wouldn't have been the best candidate for a donor anyway. Your mother's kidney disease is most likely hereditary and we prefer donors with no family history of disease. Does Sebastian's father have any history of kidney disease in his family?"

Barely able to form the word, Carrie whispered, "No."

"Well, that's good news. I know you mentioned you were divorced. Do you think Sebastian's father would be open to donating?"

"I..." Wind whipped red curls around her face as she struggled to stand. "I don't know."

"Okay. Why don't you take some time to process this news and reach out to Sebastian's dad? We still have a few weeks before he needs to go on dialysis. That will give you time to explore your options."

"I'll do that. Thank you, Dr. Stevens."

"We have a great set of counselors we can recommend, Carrie. You don't have to go through this alone. I'll have my office manager email them to you."

"Thank you. That's very kind."

"Of course. Call me when you have an update. Tell the front desk to put you straight through. Unless I'm in an urgent appointment, I'll take the call. Speak to you soon."

The phone clicked and the screen went dark, mirroring Carrie's internal mood. Barely able to move, she pulled open the door and stepped inside the office. Only making it a few feet, she collapsed by the front desk and curled up into a ball, burying her face in her thighs as she wept.

"Whoa, what's going on?" Scott's concerned voice said above her before he crouched down and wrapped his arms around her. "Hey. It's okay, Carrie. I've got you."

"Oh my god, Scott. He's going to hate me and my baby's going to die. Why is this happening?"

"Shhh..." he said, picking her up and carrying her to his office before plopping them on the leather couch. He'd carried her a few times before, mostly in high school when she'd fallen on the soccer field. She'd always been a bit clumsy and Scott was a good friend who had a slight knight in shining armor complex. He'd always nursed her and Tina's injuries and been so thoughtful. When Tina and their daughter had passed away, Carrie had done her best to return the favor and console him. They had a close friendship and she enjoyed her job as his executive assistant, understanding he paid her way too much for someone with an associate's degree and no former experience. But that was Scott and she was immensely thankful for his generous spirit.

"Here," he said, striding to grab the tissues from his desk before sitting beside her. "Blow it out and then tell me why everyone is dying."

Laughing through her tears, she wiped her nose. "Only you could break it down so acerbically, Scott. Nice job."

His lips formed a pout. "Ashlyn says I'm not nearly as surly since we got married. Don't I get a little credit?"

"You're still pretty surly," she teased, "but we love you anyway."

"Thanks." Giving a playful eye roll, he brushed her hair off her shoulder. "Is this about Sebastian's health issues?"

Nodding, she wondered where to begin. She'd never told anyone her most deeply guarded secret but if she was going to divulge it, Scott was the right person.

"Our blood types don't match so I can't donate."

"That really sucks. And I can see how it makes things worse since you'll have to contact Jeff to see if he's a match. I know you never wanted to speak to him again."

Inhaling a deep breath, she pursed her lips. "I don't need to call Jeff."

"Because you think he won't consider donating?"

"Because..." Wiping her nose, she blurted out the truth she'd hidden for so long. "Because he's not Sebastian's father."

Scott's eyes grew wide as he stared at her in disbelief. "He's not?"

"No."

Brown eyes darted between hers. "Who's the father, Carrie?"

Feeling her chin warble, she struggled to speak.

"Holy shit," he whispered.

Burying her face in her hands, she fought the onslaught of tears. Scott expelled a breath beside her and threw his head back on the couch, staring at the ceiling.

"Holy fucking shit, Carrie. Wow. I did *not* see that coming."

"It was that last time before he left, all those years ago when we got in the big fight. Remember?"

"Yep. I thought you two would never speak again. You were a wreck."

"He'd come home for Christmas to visit his mom and he showed up at my apartment. Jeff was on the hunting trip he always attended with his buddies the weekend after Christmas. Peter wanted me to break up with Jeff, and I told him I wouldn't do it unless he stayed in Ardor Creek and made a commitment. I was ready for marriage and kids and, well, he wasn't. He never has been."

"I didn't realize you two had sex during that encounter," Scott said, lifting a brow.

"What can I say?" She shrugged. "Our chemistry was always combustible. There was no denying that. The next morning, he told me it was a mistake and I should marry Jeff. Then he left and we didn't speak for seven years."

"Until he moved home and went to rehab."

"Yep. He came to me on his apology tour and I was still so angry. I wanted to tell him to fuck off. But, well, I'd made mistakes too, so I forgave him and we started over."

"Mistakes, like, you didn't tell him Sebastian was his son?" Scott asked in a droll tone.

Shooting him a glare, she lifted her hands. "What should I have done? The man was adamant he didn't want me and he never wanted kids. As soon as I took the pregnancy test and it was positive, I married Jeff and took it as a sign I was supposed to be with him."

"Are you sure Sebastian isn't Jeff's?"

Nodding, she stared at her fingers fidgeting in her lap. "I did a paternity test just to be sure when Sebastian was young. Plus, he looks like Peter. Now that you know, you see it, right?"

Scott's eyes narrowed. "The dirty blond hair and blue-green eyes. Charlie is brown-haired and brown-eyed like Jeff."

"Yep. I don't think anyone ever questioned Sebastian's coloring because I'm so fair. But so is Peter. He's pretty much the Daniel Craig of Ardor Creek. Maybe that's why I fell head over heels in love with him at first sight."

Blowing a breath through puffed cheeks, Scott studied her. "So, what are you going to do now?"

"I have to tell him. If there's even a small chance he'll donate a kidney and Dr. Stevens says he's a good match, I have to see if he'll consider it."

"Peter loves your boys, Carrie. And I know he loves you. I think he'd do it for you in a heartbeat."

"I hope so. Man, he's going to be so mad at me. I'll take every bit of anger he throws my way if he agrees to help Sebastian. I just don't care."

"He'll be mad at first but Peter's also pretty levelheaded. If you explain why you kept it from him, I have no doubt he'll try to see it from your perspective too."

"He was so awful to me the last time he left, Scott," she said, wiping a tear from her face. "He said so many hurtful things. I just couldn't bring myself to tell him, knowing he hated me that much."

"He *never* hated you, Carrie. He hated himself. That was evident in the way he almost killed himself when he lived in the city. The turnaround he's made is unbelievable and he's in a much better position to discuss your issues on a rational level. Take it from me, therapy does wonders. It saved me from almost fucking up my relationship with Ashlyn. Thank goodness I'd done the work by the time she showed up and knocked my socks off. Well, most of the work," he said, giving a sheepish grin.

"Peter has changed," she said, using a fresh tissue to wipe away the remaining tears. "He's such a different person but still the man I loved all those years ago."

"Whom you still love," he said, squeezing her hand.

"Always." Her lips formed a smile. "I'll try to remember my fondness for him when he's cursing me out."

"Peter does have a temper but I've rarely seen him use it on you."

"Oh, I've seen it. But I'm also tough and ready for a fight. When my baby's involved, I'll fight to the death." Standing, she ran her hand through her curls, shoving them from her face.

"Okay," Scott said, rising and cupping her shoulders. "Let's hope it doesn't get *that* far. Maybe just a good ol' fashioned blow out will suffice before you both move on and help Sebastian."

"I hope so."

His lips formed a goofy smile and she craned her neck.

"Scott?"

"I might have a secret to tell you too. I think Ashlyn will be okay with me telling you first."

"*Ohmygod*, Scott!" she shrieked, pasting her hands to her cheeks and jumping up and down. "You guys are pregnant!"

"We're pregnant," he said, chuckling. "She's twelve weeks and we just decided to start telling people."

Throwing her arms around him, she squeezed for dear life. "I'm so happy for you! You must be so thrilled." Drawing back, she rubbed his arms. "Are you handling it okay? It must make you think of Ella and Tina."

"It does but in a good way," he said, leaning on his desk as his expression grew pensive. "I've convinced myself they'd want me to be happy and Ashlyn is so damn understanding. She's adamant we tell Ella's brother or sister everything about her and her mom. I have no idea what I did to deserve her. She's amazing."

"She is and so are you, my friend. I couldn't be more excited for you. I want to throw Ashlyn's shower. Do you think she'd be open to that?"

"I'll ask her. I know she has some good friends in the city but she wants to have it here and you're her best friend in Ardor Creek, so it will probably make her ecstatic."

"Awesome. I'm so glad she considers me her best friend here. I love her so much, Scott. Plus, I'm just excited you married someone who loves karaoke. She's my favorite duet partner."

"Besides Peter."

"Besides Peter," she sighed. "I knew during our first church choir duet in tenth grade he'd be my karaoke partner for life."

"Who knows? Maybe this news could shift something in your relationship and you could try again. I always wondered why you didn't give it a go when he moved back to Ardor Creek."

"Because I was still married and he was a shell of a man hanging on by a thread."

"But you're none of those things anymore," he said, holding up a finger.

"No, I'm just the woman who always represented everything he despised and now I'll be the woman who kept his child from him.

Not really a blazing endorsement. I think I'll keep that off my Match.com profile."

Huffing a laugh, Scott lifted a shoulder. "You never know. Let's revisit this discussion in a few months. For now, you need to tell him and get Sebastian healthy."

"Damn straight."

Scott's eyebrows drew together. "You know, Ashlyn and I will just be hanging at home on Thursday and Friday night. Why don't you see when Peter's available to talk and we'll watch the boys? They seem enthralled with the attic and everything Sally Pickens. It will be fun and will give you guys the privacy you need."

"They don't call you the saint of Ardor Creek for nothing," she said, kissing his cheek before wiping away the gloss. "I'll see what night he's available and let you know. Thanks."

"Sure thing. It will all work out, Carrie. You'll see."

Giving her friend one last hug, she hoped like hell the words were true.

Chapter 5

♥

Thursday evening, Carrie stirred the turkey chili, wishing she could stir away the dread in her gut. She used to make the meal when Peter would come home from the city during those first years after he left. It was a simple recipe and represented comfort food for both of them. He would return to Ardor Creek to visit his mom, who was living alone after Peter's dad passed away from liver failure.

Carrie had finished her associate's degree at the local community college and worked as a waitress until she could find more stable employment. The tiny apartment she lived in was sparse but it was home. She'd moved out from under her parents' thumb and it was liberating. Although Carrie believed in the teachings of the church, she considered herself more spiritual than religious. Her father hated that, of course, which led to their relationship being strained.

Peter would come to town in his flashy cars, full of zeal for the life he was building in Manhattan. He'd worked his way up to partner in a fancy investment firm and would zip through town on the quick visits. Each time, he'd ask to stop by her apartment and see her and since she was still in love with him, she could never say no. Even though he'd broken her fragile heart so many times.

Sighing, she sprinkled chili powder into the large pot and covered it, letting it simmer. Taking a sip of pinot grigio, she told herself to stay calm. Peter didn't have the ability to break her heart anymore. She'd steeled herself against that long ago.

Remembering the very first time he'd shattered her, Carrie relaxed in the kitchen chair and let the memories wash over her.

"I'm moving to Manhattan, Carrie," Peter said as they sat beside the lake, shivering under the September night sky. "Now that I have my bachelor's degree, I'm going to get my CPA and complete the Series 7 exam. I won't stop until I'm running the largest financial firm in the city."

Tears burned her eyes, the words confirming he coveted those things above building a life with her. "I wish you'd stay here but I know you're miserable. I thought I made you happy but I guess I don't."

"You're the only thing here that makes me happy," he said, lacing their fingers and squeezing. "I want you to come with me."

Scoffing, she pulled her hand away. "To New York? I wouldn't know the first thing about living there. Ardor Creek is my home. I want to build a family here and raise children who love all the things I loved as a kid. The fall festival, the Christmas parade, the church picnics..."

"Well, that's great, but your dad banned me from church so I don't really have the same fondness you do."

Carrie rolled her eyes. "He banned you because he thinks he can control me. I have my own apartment now and he can screw himself."

"Blasphemy," Peter teased, butting her with his shoulder. "God might strike you down." He pointed to the sky.

"God knows living with them was torture. I think he'll give me a pass."

"Our parents suck." He kicked the grass with his toe. "Your dad thinks I'm a degenerate and not good enough to be within fifty feet of you, and my dad..." Gazing at his arm, he ran his fingers over the old scars, causing sympathy to well in Carrie's heart. "Well, he thinks a twelve-year-old boy is an ashtray. Fucking asshole. Can't wait until he croaks and leaves me and Mom in peace."

"He's an ass for sure," she said, tracing the scars, hating he'd been hurt by someone who was supposed to love him. "But you eventually grew old enough to fight back and he never touched you again."

"Damn straight. I'd kill him if I didn't think it would break Mom's heart. She still loves him for some reason."

"Some people can't control who they love," she said, gazing into his eyes. "I never could. I still can't. Even though you're going to leave me."

"Come with me," he urged, turning to face her. Wrapping his legs around her hips, he pulled her into the juncture of his thighs. Straddling each other on the soft grass, they exchanged lazy kisses before Carrie drew back.

"I don't want that life, Peter," she whispered, running her thumb over his lip. "I want a family and kids and a home in Ardor Creek. Those are my dreams. I thought they were yours too. I wish I was enough for you to stay."

"I love you, Carrie," he said, reverent in the moonlight. "But I hate this place. Your parents detest me and will never accept me. And I need to prove myself. To make something of myself so I'm not Arnold Stratford's degenerate son. That's how everyone sees me here."

"I don't see you that way."

"You're the only one."

Silence stretched as they contemplated the ramifications of the intense conversation.

"Maybe after a few years, once you go build something, you'll come back and marry me and we can start a family."

Expelling a breath, he shook his head. "And tie myself to Ardor Creek forever? No way. I'm not creating a scenario that forces me to stay here. Not now, not ever."

"So, what does that mean?" she asked, sliding back so she was free of his embrace. "You're done with me? You're moving on and you don't want me anymore?"

"I want you so much, honey—"

"But not enough to stay," she interrupted, lifting her chin, feeling the fury ignite deep in her belly.

Blue eyes glimmered with regret and sorrow. "But not enough to stay," he said softly.

Standing, she jutted her finger in his face as anger began to fill his expression. "You're an ass, Peter Stratford! I gave you everything and you're exactly the person my dad said you were. You got into my pants years ago and now you're tossing me away like some dirty secret you're ashamed of."

"I'm not ashamed of you," he said, standing and knocking her hand away. "I'm ashamed of myself, Carrie! Can't you understand that? I let that bastard abuse us for years and haven't done one damn thing I'm proud of. I need to make something of myself. To become someone your dad will accept. Hell, someone that everyone in this podunk town will accept. You'll never understand what it's like to be the town degenerate because everyone loves you. Perfect Carrie Longwood, the preacher's daughter. You have no idea what it's like to be hated and to hate yourself."

"I know what it means to love someone and it doesn't look like this." She gestured between them. "I don't care what other people think. I would be proud to be your wife and to have you as the father of my children."

Palming his forehead, he groaned. "I told you, I don't want that. We're twenty-two, Carrie. We have our whole lives ahead of us."

"You just want to screw other women and be with other people more exciting than me. Admit it."

"Good grief. Are you really going there? This has nothing to do with that."

"But you're curious," she said, eyes welling with tears. "Admit it. We've only ever been with each other. I'm not enough for you."

Slowly advancing, he cupped her face. "Carrie, I think it would be disingenuous if we both didn't admit we're a little curious what sex would be like with someone else. That doesn't mean we don't love each other. It's just human."

"I'm not curious."

"That's ridiculous," he said, frustrated.

"You're ridiculous," she said, shoving his chest. "So fine! Go and screw a thousand other women for all I care. You've obviously decided I'm not worth your precious time. I hope you become rich and conquer the world, and one day you'll realize you gave up the best thing you ever had!" Pivoting, she stomped toward their cars, unable to gaze upon his handsome face, knowing he didn't want her. Didn't love her.

"Carrie," he said, grabbing her arm.

"No!" Whirling around, she stuck a finger in his face. "Don't draw this out. If you're done with me, then go." She pointed to his jeep, parked beside her hatchback. "At least you can be man enough to make a clean break."

"Honey..." he pleaded, encircling her wrists.

"No," she said, tugging her arms free. "Choose me or leave, Peter. It's up to you."

They stood frozen for so long, she wondered if they might turn to stone. Eventually, he gave her one last, long glare—full of sentiment and remorse—and strode to his car. Bright lights flooded the darkness before he pulled away, gravel shifting underneath his tires.

Left alone, as she would always be by Peter, she crumbled to the ground and released every tear until they dried. And then, she drove home to begin her life without him.

A knock sounded at the front door, jarring Carrie from the memory.

"Carrie? You in the kitchen?" Peter's deep voice chimed.

Clearing her throat, she stood and headed over to check on the chili. "Yep! Come on back."

"Smells like turkey chili," he said, handsome as a movie star as he strolled into the kitchen. "My favorite," he said, running his hand over her shoulder as she stirred the contents of the pot.

"It will be ready soon. We can eat in here or on the porch. It's pretty warm tonight. Whatever you want."

"Doesn't matter to me," he said, his eyes darting over her face. "I was pretty surprised to get an invitation on a night the boys weren't here. You don't really hang out with me alone anymore."

Shrugging, she was thankful he removed his hand since it caused her skin to burn underneath her shirt. She'd always been insanely attracted to Peter, even now that he was pushing forty. How unfair that he'd become more handsome as he aged. Bastard.

"It will be nice. Like old times before you left and didn't look back."

His brows lifted. "Is that a dig? I think it's a dig."

"It's just the truth," she said, setting down the spoon and opening the cabinet beside the stove. Grabbing two bowls, she set them on the small island behind her. "Grab the shredded cheese and sour cream from the fridge."

"Yes ma'am," he said, opening the refrigerator and pulling them out. "Anything else?"

"Nope, that's good." Gesturing to the pot, she said, "Spoon out what you want and I'll grab mine and we can eat on the porch."

As he scooped the chili into his bowl, Carrie grabbed her wine, all but chugging the remaining liquid. Telling herself to be strong, she prepared herself to inform the man who'd never wanted children about his son.

Chapter 6

♥

Peter sat in the wooden rocker on Carrie's front porch, realizing he was being buttered up for something. Turkey chili was their go-to all those years ago when he would visit her in the tiny apartment during his trips home. Each time, she would ask him to stay—whether it be with her words or with her eyes—and every time he would leave like the heartless bastard he was.

It had never been about his feelings for her. His love for her was the one unfailing constant that had always defined his life. But she also embodied and embraced Ardor Creek, and that meant she represented everything Peter detested. His shitbag father, his mother's unwillingness to leave him, the disdain that Pastor Longwood felt toward him. Carrie somehow became the manifestation of all that pain and he'd punished her for it. She'd never deserved one ounce of the anguish he'd caused her, and he ached with so much regret, he wondered if he might drown in it one day.

She'd forgiven him three years ago, even though he'd been sure she would reject him. After all, he'd rejected her so many times, he'd almost hoped she'd toss his apology in his face. But she'd handled it with the grace she'd always possessed and accepted him back into her life. Not into heart—he would never deserve that—but he was so damn thankful to be in her life.

Still, hc kncw Carrie better than anyone on Earth and something was up. All the signs were present she wanted to have a private conversation with him. Wondering what the hell she wanted to discuss, he racked his brain. No way in hell did she call him over to ask him to try again. Peter would never delude himself she'd ever offer her love again. He'd fucked that up royally. Chewing the delicious chili, he drifted into the memory of their last blowout over a decade ago…

"What are you doing here, Peter?" Carrie asked, cheeks flushed as she stood in the doorway. "Jeff is gone on his hunting trip and you should be with your mom."

"Mom's fine," he said, stepping inside. "I needed to see you."

Her features scrunched. "You're drunk. Did you drive over here? I can't believe how irresponsible you are. Get inside so I can make you some coffee."

He shuffled in, ashamed at her scolding, knowing she was right. But the thing was, when you were the son of a degenerate alcoholic, it turned out you had the propensity to become one yourself. Add in the cocaine, ecstasy, and expensive call girls, and he was a scourge on society.

"Sit on the couch," she said, directing him to the soft plush. "I'll be back in a minute."

He relaxed into the cushions, wondering what the hell he was going to say. All he knew was that he'd come home for Christmas and heard from everyone in Ardor Creek that Carrie was about to marry Jeff Lawrence. He'd moved into town a year ago and had apparently swept her off her feet.

"Bastard," he muttered, running his hand over his face. Carrie was his. Didn't that asshole understand? Once he was ready, he'd convince her to move into the city and finally give her the kids she wanted. They would compromise and find a way.

"Here," she said, thrusting the mug in his face. "Drink and then tell me why you think you can show up at my place, drunk and belligerent."

Peter sipped, scowling at the burn on his tongue. "It's hot."

"It's coffee, you idiot."

Glaring at her, he blew on the liquid before taking another sip. They sat in silence as he drank, formulating the words he needed to say. Setting the half-empty cup on the side table, he turned to face her.

"You can't marry him, Carrie. He's an asshole."

Scoffing, her mouth fell open. "As opposed to you?"

"Terry said he comes into the pub on nights you volunteer at the community center and hits on other women. One night, she said he left with one. Are you really going to marry a guy who does that?"

Bristling, she asked, "How dare you come into town for two days and think you know anything about me or the man I'm dating? You're the one who left, remember? I happen to love Jeff and know exactly what he's doing. Sometimes he drives people home when they've had too much to drink. He always lets me know when he'll be late."

"Wow. So, as long as he texts you that he's fucking someone else, that's fine? Are you serious, Carrie?"

"How dare you?" Fists formed so tight he wondered if her nails pierced the skin of her palms. "You have no right—"

"I have every right!" he screamed, shoving a finger in her face. "You're mine, Carrie. It's time we figured out how to make this work."

Eyes widening, she stared at him in disbelief. "How to make what work? You left me, Peter! Years ago. I wasn't exciting enough for your city life. What do you possibly think we still have?"

"We still love each other," he said, desperation setting in. "I still love you, Carrie."

"So what? Did that stop you from leaving? From screwing god knows how many women in the city? You must be so happy you sowed your oats and got your kicks since I was never enough."

"You were always enough," he said, feeling tears form in his eyes like a fucking sap. "I was just so broken. You never understood that."

"You were never broken to me but that never mattered to you."

"It mattered," he said, scooting toward her and cupping her cheeks. "It still matters. Let me try to earn you."

"How?" she whispered, shaking her head. "It's over for us, Peter."

"I'll give you kids," he said, desperate to say anything to ensure she didn't marry someone else. "We can live in the city and raise them there. I have a huge penthouse. You'll love it."

"I love Ardor Creek. It's the only place I want to raise kids."

Groaning in frustration, he rolled his eyes. "What is your obsession with this place? I hate it here."

"That's not a newsflash, Peter. You always have. Which is why I don't understand why you're here. We want different things in life."

"I think I could have kids with you, Carrie. I don't hate the idea. I just don't want to raise them here."

"Then we have nothing to talk about." Disengaging from his grasp, she stood and walked to the window. "I wish I could try living in the city. Sometimes I tell myself it's my fault because I never considered moving with you. But I knew I wouldn't be happy there."

"Even if you were with me?" he asked, walking toward her and cupping her shoulders. Pulling her body into his, he buried his face in her hair. "Please don't give up on us. I can't live with myself if you marry him."

Her nostrils flared in the reflection of the window as she digested his words. Turning in his arms, she slid her hands behind his neck. "All I ever wanted was a promise you'd stay and love me back."

"I do love you," he whispered, resting his forehead against hers.

"But will you stay?"

"Yes." The lie left his lips easily, reminding him what a jerk he truly was. "I'll stay. Please, Carrie. Don't marry him."

"Peter..."

Devouring her lips, he kissed her as if he was going off to war, never to be heard from again. Lifting her in his arms, he carried her to the bedroom, tearing off their clothes before they loved each other, clinging and desperate.

In the morning, when the sun shone through the slit in the bedroom window and Peter was stone-cold sober, he awoke with her in his arms. Terror shot down his spine as the rest of his life flashed before his eyes. Every day, stuck in Ardor Creek, away from the fast-paced world of drugs and money he now coveted. Awash with the knowledge of promises he'd made, he extricated from her embrace and dressed.

After chugging two glasses of water in the kitchen, he returned with one for her. She slept so peacefully, red hair strewn over every inch of the pillow. Racked with pain, he touched her bare shoulder and gently shook her awake. Her smile was bright as he loomed above her, sitting on the side of the bed. Brighter than he deserved, especially since he knew he was about to leave her once again.

"Here," he said, gesturing with the glass. "I brought you some water."

"You're already dressed," she said, eyeing him warily as she sat up and took the glass. Taking a gulp, she set it on the bedside table. "You're heading back to your mom's?"

"I'm heading back to the city."

Her expression collapsed into one of such pain, he wished for a knife so he could plunge it into his own heart.

"No, you're not," she whispered.

"I have to."

"But you said...I thought you were open..."

In truth, he was so close to being open to staying and giving her the family she wanted but he knew it would be a disservice. He was a coked-out junkie with a multitude of addictions that needed addressing before he would even consider being a father. Otherwise, he'd be no better than his shithead old man.

"I'm an addict, Carrie. Just like he was. A drunk and a reprobate."

"We'll get you into rehab, then."

"I'm not ready, Care Bear. I might never be."

"You promised," she said, a tear skating down her cheek as his heart exploded.

"I'm sorry." Lifting his hand, he stroked the tear.

Anger flashed in her eyes and she swatted his hand away. "Get out."

"I don't want to fight, Carrie."

"Get the fuck out," she screamed, holding the sheet to her chest as she pointed to the door. "I never want to see you again!"

Standing, he showed her his palms. "I'll call you once you've calmed down—"

"Calmed down, my ass," she said, standing and wrapping the sheet around her body. Holding it in place, she grabbed the half-empty glass. "Get the fuck out, Peter!"

In that moment, he understood what he had to do. Keeping the tether between them would always lead them here, to this place that held so much pain and heartache. It was the inevitable conclusion for two people who wanted such vastly different things.

"I was wrong. You should marry Jeff. Have the kids and the marriage you've always wanted. I can't give you those things."

"But you could fuck me one last time, right?" Launching the glass at him, he ducked before it shattered against the wall.

"Jesus, Carrie! You almost hit me."

"I fucking hate you," she said, rushing him and beating him with her fists. "I hate you so much."

"I hate you too!" he hissed, his tone nasty as he grabbed her upper arms. "I hate you for asking me to stay here in this pissant town and asking me to settle for a life that will make me miserable!"

Her features contorted with pain. "You don't know the first thing about loving someone. You disgust me."

"Well, you're no saint either, Carrie. I'm pretty sure you're not going to tell your fiancé you fucked around with your scumbag ex, so screw you and your holier than thou judgement. You're no better than your father."

"Get out!"

"He'll never fuck you like I do," he whispered, hating himself but knowing it would cement her decision to move on. As much as he loathed imagining her with anyone else, he couldn't give her what she needed. "Think of me while he tries to make you come." Releasing her, he stormed from the room and out the front door, hearing her frustrated scream before slamming it behind him.

He made it a mile in his rented luxury Mercedes before he pulled over and puked his guts out, hands resting on his knees as he retched. Sick from the cruel words he'd spoken, he almost turned back to beg for her forgiveness. But that would lead them back to the same place. He and Carrie always ended up in the same agonizing place. Deciding to do what was best for her for once in his damn life, he drove back to the city and drowned himself in tequila and cocaine.

"Earth to Peter," Carrie called, jarring him from the terrible memory. "Where did you go?"

"I'm here," he said, scooping up the last bite of chili. "It tastes better than ever."

"I've been putting more hot sauce in it lately. The boys actually like spicy stuff and you know I do too."

"Maybe it's the red hair. They say redheads are spicy." He waggled his brows.

"Do they?" she asked, glancing at the porch ceiling. "Maybe. I've always thought I was pretty middle of the road. Maybe even boring." She gave him a sad smile.

"You're not boring, honey," he said, setting his bowl on the little table beside the chair. "Anyone who thinks that is just really fucked up. You're amazing and gorgeous and strong."

"I'm pretty sure you thought I was boring for a long time."

"Like I said, really fucked up." He tapped his temple with his finger. "I still wonder how much of it is scrambled from all the shit I stuffed up my nose."

Squishing her features, she shrugged. "You only seem mildly fucked up to me."

"Then we've come a long way," he said, chuckling.

"We have. I'm so glad we're in a better place, Peter."

"Me too, honey. You have no idea."

Biting her lip, she looked pensive and his heart began to pound.

"What is it, Carrie? I know you didn't bring me here for shits and giggles. There must be a reason you wanted to speak to me alone."

Lifting her chin, she nodded. "There is but I need another glass of wine. Let's talk in the living room. It's getting chilly."

"Okay," he said, standing and stacking their bowls. He followed her inside, still obsessed with her cute little ass inside her tight jeans, even after all these years. Feeling himself harden, he told himself to calm down. Their relationship wasn't sexual anymore and it never would be again. He'd lost that privilege and mourned it every night he clutched his pillow, wishing it was her soft body against him. Handing her the bowls, she rinsed them and put them in the dishwasher before refilling her wine glass.

"Ready?" she asked, gesturing toward the living room.

"Ready," he said, placing his hand on her lower back and urging her to lead. Following her into the living room, he sat on the couch beside her. "I'm rapt with anticipation here, honey."

"Well, get ready, because I've got a doozy."

Straightening his spine, he studied her, wondering why he felt his life was about to inexorably change.

Chapter 7

C arrie chugged a huge gulp of wine as she prepared herself for the inevitable argument. They hadn't argued for so long but he was going to be angry and she was ready to let him rail. Once they had it out, she'd ask him to move on and hopefully help Sebastian. Her son was all that mattered.

"Are you trying to get drunk before you tell me?" he teased, lifting his brows.

"Maybe," she said, hiccupping. Realizing she needed a clear head, she set the glass on the side table before facing him. Licking her lips, she inhaled a huge breath. "I'm not a match to donate to Sebastian."

"Oh, honey, I'm so sorry," he said, scooting closer and taking her hand. "I know you wanted to donate so badly. Is it because of your mom's history of kidney disease?"

"That and other things."

"What other things?"

"Sebastian and I have different blood types. I'm A and he's O. He needs a donor who also has O blood."

"Man, that's rough. You're going to have to contact Jeff. I know you wanted nothing to do with him now that he's in Colorado with the new wife and kid, although he should be paying you child support."

"Zero child support in exchange for his dismissal of custody is a perfect arrangement in my mind. I don't want the boys anywhere near him."

Concern entered his gaze. "I know he cheated on you, fucking scumbag. Did he ever hurt the boys?"

Sighing, she nodded. "He became rough with them as they grew older. I was willing to overlook the cheating for a while because I felt they needed a father."

"That's ridiculous. You never should've stayed with him."

"It's easy to say when you don't have kids to think about. Regardless, it never really mattered to me. I hadn't been attracted to him for years and honestly didn't give a shit he was with other women. It saved me from having to fake it."

"That's awful," Peter whispered. "I all but pushed you into that jerk's arms. I hate myself for it, Carrie."

"It doesn't matter anymore. He's gone and he'll never hurt my babies again. He slapped Charlie across the face one day when he knocked over a jug of Kool-Aid. He'd told the boys to stop throwing the ball around the kitchen but they continued as rambunctious kids do. The ball hit the jug and it splattered everywhere. Jeff slapped him so hard, I felt my heart lurch from my chest. God, Peter, I wanted to kill him."

"Bastard," he said, shaking his head as he stroked her hand. "I wish I had been there."

"I took out a restraining order that day. Stuffed the boys in the car and drove to the station and Gary filled everything out. He followed me home and made sure Jeff moved out. Of course, he moved right in with his twenty-five-year-old flame and proceeded to knock her up. Thank god they moved to Colorado. I hate him, Peter."

His thumb skated over her skin as he contemplated. "But now you have to contact him to see if he can help Sebastian. Man, life isn't fair. Is that why you wanted to speak to me? Do you want me to help you in the process of contacting him? Anything you need, Carrie. All you have to do is ask."

Cupping his cheek, she smoothed her thumb over his stubble. "I hope that's true."

"Of course, it is," he said, giving her that goofy grin she'd always adored. "You finally need me at a time when I'm stuck in Ardor Creek, whether I like it or not."

Laughing, she bit her lip. "Do you hate it as much as you thought?"

"Honestly, I don't. I mean, I miss the city, but living there isn't conducive to my sobriety. We both know that. Moving back here and living with Mom was the best option. Now that she's gone, I try to embrace living in her house and being the town accountant. Working with Scott at GDC has been really good for me too. I love negotiating all of the investor and corporate contracts for him. It's not terrible, especially since you and I are in such a good place."

Covering her hand upon his face, he gazed at her and spoke so reverently. "I missed you so much, Carrie. All those years. I wish I had been a better man for you."

"I know that now," she said as tears stung her eyes. "I made mistakes too."

"No, you didn't. I accept responsibility. That was an important part of my recovery. Accepting responsibility for my transgressions and lies, both to myself and to everyone else."

"I lied too, Peter."

His eyebrows drew together. "When did you lie?"

Her chest rose and fell with each bated breath. "I don't need to contact Jeff about the transplant."

Confusion laced his blue eyes. "Don't you want to see if he's open to donating?"

Her irises darted over his face, memorizing every feature one last time before everything changed. "Remember when you said you didn't know your blood type?"

His brow furrowed. "Yeah."

"I'm pretty sure I know what it is," she whispered.

Comprehension entered his gaze as his breathing escalated, forming short pants as he contemplated her. "What are you saying?"

"I'm pretty sure your blood type is O like Sebastian's."

Pulling away from her touch, he straightened.

"Carrie...?" His tone was incredulous as he shook his head, anger and betrayal strewn over his features. "It's not true..."

"It is," she said, closing her eyes as a tear slid down her cheek. "I'm so sorry." Lifting her lids, she prepared for his wrath. "I never knew how to tell you. You were so awful to me the last time you left and swore you never wanted kids."

"So you passed my kid off as Jeff's?" he screamed, standing and extending his hands at his sides in exasperation. "You couldn't bring yourself to tell me I had a son?"

"After you said awful things to me and left me for the hundredth time?" she yelled, standing and glaring at him. "I wasn't about to embark on a fireside chat about how you knocked me up, no. Sorry if that didn't work for your schedule, Mr. Big City Slicker."

"For Christ's sake, Carrie! Of course, I would've wanted to know you were pregnant with my child. I would've come home and made things right. I would've married you!"

"And hated me forever? No thanks. I wasn't signing either of us up for that life. Not then, not now, not ever."

"Fuck, Carrie, you're a real asshole for keeping this from me. I can't believe you!"

"I'll never be as big an asshole as you!" she screamed, spittle flying from her lips. "You made it clear you didn't want anything to do with me, and I assumed that sentiment also included our child. If you want to blame me, that's fine, but it doesn't change the fact he's sick and he needs a kidney. I know this sucks, and we can fight all day long for all I care, but I need to know if you'll consider donating, Peter."

"Are you even sorry?" he asked, his eyes threatening to bug out of his head. "Do you even care that you lied to me for ten fucking years?"

"Stop screaming at me!"

He opened his mouth and she was sure he was about to unleash a tirade of curses at her, but at the last moment, he expelled a breath, cheeks puffing as his shoulders deflated.

"Good god, Carrie. I told myself I would never argue like this with you again. It's so fucking corrosive. I can't do it. It dredges up all the old anger and makes the addict inside surge. Just let me breathe for a damn second."

Exhaling her own rush of air, she waited, blood coursing through her body as she observed him pace across the rug. Finally, he swiped a hand through his dark blond hair and lifted his gaze to hers.

"I'm furious right now. I need you to know that because I'm not going to show it in the old ways that were so toxic. Got it?"

Nodding, she squared her shoulders. "Got it."

"Okay. I need some time to process this but, unfortunately, we don't have a lot of time where Sebastian is concerned, right?"

"If he doesn't get a transplant by mid-May, he's going to have to go on dialysis." Feeling her chin warble, she buried her face in her hands. "I just want to help my baby," she cried, devolving into tears and collapsing on the couch.

Sighing, he slid beside her, pulling her into his arms and stroking her hair as she wept upon his chest. "I know, honey. I want to help him too. Please don't cry." Kissing her hair, he stroked her as she unleashed all her pain and regret.

"Look at me," he finally said, lifting her chin with his fingers once her tears began to abate. "You don't need to cry, hon. Of course, I'll donate a kidney to Sebastian."

Hope surged in her heart. "You will?"

"Yes, Carrie," he said, placing his forehead upon hers. "I would do anything for you. It took me so long to get to a place where that was true and I'm finally able to show you. I'll do it for you and for our son." Releasing a shaky breath, he shook his head. "Holy shit. I can't believe he's our son."

"I'm so sorry," she whispered, caressing his face. "Please don't hate me."

"I could never hate you," he said, brushing a kiss across her lips. "I love you with my entire soul. Don't you know that?"

"It's never been true," she said against his lips.

"It's *always* been true." Thrusting his fingers in her hair, he pulled her tight into his body. "I just never deserved you and I sure as hell wasn't ready for you."

"Ready for all my dreams you detested."

"What I didn't realize for so long was that I craved those dreams too. I was just so fucked up inside I couldn't see it."

"You never wanted to be stuck here. To be stuck with me."

"Let me tell you something, Carrie, and you'd damn well better listen. Being stuck anywhere with you is my goddamn ultimate fantasy. Do you hear me?"

Carrie stroked his jaw, studying him in the dim light of the lamp as their breaths mingled.

"I don't believe you."

"That doesn't make it less true," he said, sliding his hand to cup her ass. God, she'd missed those broad hands on every inch of her body and shimmied into him, eliciting a deep growl from his chest. Reveling in the sexy sound, she felt a rush of moisture between her thighs.

"*Peter...*"

"*Fuck*," he whispered before closing his lips over hers. Sliding her hand into his thick hair, she clutched on for dear life and welcomed his wet tongue inside her mouth.

Chapter 8

Peter devoured Carrie's lips, disbelief coursing through him at the fact he was holding her again...touching her again while she squirmed in his arms. Her lithe body writhed atop his as she slid over his crotch, straddling him as she maneuvered against him. Their spark had always been undeniable, and she'd always undulated into him when they loved each other, stemming from her need to be as close as possible. He felt the same, striving to eradicate every open space between them as he drew her close, spearing his tongue into her mouth as he cupped the gorgeous mounds of her ass.

Her sexy purrs set him on fire and he rewarded her by drawing her tongue between his lips. As he sucked her wet tongue, he pushed his erection into her crotch, dying to surge inside her tight warmth. Clenching his hair, she dry humped him, reminding him of all the times they'd done this before they finally lost their virginity to each other. Dating the preacher's daughter had led to a shit ton of dry humping but he'd never minded with Carrie. His gorgeous, magnificent Carrie. Every opportunity to touch her had been heaven.

"More," she cried before tugging her shirt over her head. Cementing her lips back to his, she pleaded, "Please, Peter."

Unclasping her bra, he tugged it from her body, shuddering at the sight of her pert breasts. Pebbled nipples strained toward him and he captured one in his mouth, rolling it on his tongue as she arched her back. Silky hair caressed his arm, flowing from her lolling crown. Beautiful as a mermaid rising from the ocean, she quivered atop his vibrating frame. Dying to make her scream—in pleasure rather than anger—he flicked her nipple with his tongue before sucking it between his lips.

"Oh, god," she moaned, shoving her breast into his mouth, reminding him how insatiable she was in bed. She'd always been a passionate lover and he longed to excite her even half as much as she turned him on. Trailing kisses to her other breast, he drew the tight bud into his mouth, closing his eyes as the joy of caressing her overwhelmed him.

"Touch my pussy," she cried, unbuttoning her jeans and giving a frustrated grunt when she couldn't gain access. Sliding off his thighs, she tugged them off, along with her underwear. "Yours too," she said, reaching for his fly.

"Carrie," he said, clutching her hand atop his massive erection. "Should we really be doing this right now?"

Lowering her lips to his, she said the six sexiest words he'd ever heard in his life. "Shut up and fuck me, Peter."

Unable to deny her, he undid his pants, watching her shimmy them and his boxers down his thighs as he pulled his shirt over his head. Straddling him, she dug her nails into his shoulders. "Do we need to use a condom?"

"I get regular checkups since rehab and everything is clean, Carrie. I promise."

"I have an IUD and nothing ever showed up on my yearly exams from that bastard, thank god."

Spearing his fingers in her hair, he growled, "Don't ever speak about him when I'm fucking you, Carrie. I mean it. He should've never touched you. You're mine."

Aligning her sopping wet core with his straining cock, she doused him with her essence, making him grit his teeth. "You had other lovers."

"I should've never been with anyone but you." Grabbing the base of his cock, he dragged the sensitive head over her opening. "No one else ever. For either of us. This is mine." Staring deep into her stunning green eyes, he surged his hips, jutting into her slick warmth as she screamed his name.

"Yes, honey," he said, drawing back through her taut, quivering folds before surging forward again. *"Mine."*

Pressing her lips to his, she plunged her tongue in his mouth, undulating her hips in the rhythm that was Carrie...only Carrie. Returning her kiss with lust-filled ardor, he gripped her ass cheeks, guiding her back and forth over his sensitive shaft as he finally returned home, to the woman he adored but certainly didn't deserve. Even with the massive secret she'd kept, his transgressions were so much worse.

"I need you to...I need..." Sliding her hand to her clit, she began to rub the sensitive spot.

"Let me take you there, honey," he whispered against her lips, dragging her hand away and replacing it with his thumb. Wanting to increase the pleasure, he slid his thumb to her core, gliding his cock out and jutting his thumb inside to coat it with her honey. Circling inside her tight channel, he gathered her juices, moistening his skin before sliding it back to her clit. Thrusting back inside her sweet pussy with his shaft, he began stimulating the swollen little bud.

Burying her face in his neck, she clutched his shoulders as he fucked her in the timeless rhythm he only had with Carrie. Pressing his lips to the shell of her ear, he spoke words of love, knowing she wouldn't believe him but needing her to know. How sorry he was...how much he adored her...how good she felt around his near to bursting cock.

Increasing the pace of his thumb on her clit, he felt her body tense and knew she was close.

"Come all over my dick, honey," he murmured in her ear. "You feel so sweet and tight around me. I missed that pretty little pussy."

She bit his neck, the little she-devil, causing him to fuck her even harder. "You're still a little bitch in bed, Carrie," he said, his balls tightening as they slapped against her slippery core. "I fucking love it. Bite me harder."

She complied, digging her nails into his shoulders as she nearly pierced his neck with her teeth.

"Fuck, I'm coming. Damn it, Carrie...I can't...*oh, god...*"

Releasing everything into her, he pinched her clit between his fingers, sending her over the edge as his body spasmed and quaked beneath her. Jets upon jets of his sticky release shot into her body as her muscles gripped him tight. Each wave of her orgasm rocked him as her swollen folds milked his shaft. Ready to die from pleasure, he breathed in her scent, rubbing his face against her soft hair. Knowing he was so damn lucky to be in her arms once again, he caressed her back with his broad hand as they both fell back to Earth. Content to remain there forever, sated and spent, he reveled in her embrace.

"Mmmm..." she moaned near his ear, causing him to shiver.

"Honey, if it ends up with you fucking me like that, I think you need to keep secrets from me more often."

Her body tensed ever so slightly before she let go, breaking into a round of joyful giggles against his neck. Laughing with her, he caressed her sweaty skin, running his fingers over her back, up to her gorgeous hair, and back down again to pat her ass.

"That wasn't part of the private discussion plan," she mumbled into his neck.

"I don't care. It was my favorite part, unplanned or not."

"Me too." She snuggled into him, familiar and intimate, and he damn near felt his heart explode. If he could hold her like this forever, it wouldn't be long enough.

Suddenly, a pair of headlights beamed through the front window and she sat up with a gasp. "Oh my god," she said, sliding off him and searching for her clothes, causing his limp cock to mourn the loss of her tight warmth. "Ashlyn will be here with the boys any minute. I told her to be back by nine." Picking up her phone from the coffee table, she checked the time.

"It's nine on the dot. Shit!" She tugged on her clothes as she gave him an exasperated glare. "Well, get dressed! I don't want them to know what we were doing!"

"They won't know, Carrie," he said, lacing his fingers behind his head. "I'm depleted over here. Give me a minute."

Grabbing his shirt from the floor, she pressed it against his chest. "Get up and get dressed right now, Peter Stratford! Do you hear me?"

Grasping her hips, he dragged her atop his body as she yelped. "God, you're so fucking cute when you're scolding me." He gave her a sloppy kiss. "Do it again."

She scrambled off and glared at him. "I mean it, Peter. Please."

The plea in her voice moved him and he rose, hating to end the intimate moment. He shrugged on his clothes not a minute too soon because ten seconds later, two boys came barreling through the front door.

"Hi, guys," Carrie said, crouching to hug them as they ran toward her. "Did you have fun with Ashlyn and Scott?"

"We had so much fun!" Charlie said. "Sally's chair rocked on its own and we also dug behind the house for treasure. Ashlyn said Sally might've buried letters behind the house."

"You never know," Ashlyn said from the doorway, shrugging. "Grandma Jean told me a lot of unverified stories. I told the boys they can help me investigate them."

"How exciting," Carrie said, kissing both their cheeks before rising to her feet.

"Did you have fun with Uncle Peter?" Sebastian asked.

"I sure did, sweetie," she said, caressing his cheek.

"Oh, it, uh, looks like Uncle Peter's fly is unzipped," Ashlyn said, brows lifted as she craned her neck. "Looks like you guys had a *lot* of fun."

"Oops," Peter said, zipping his fly and giving a sly smile.

"Oh, brother," Carrie muttered, slapping her palm to her forehead.

"Well, well. Seems like I should've been late returning the boys. Sorry I was on time."

"I'm glad you were on time. Peter was just leaving, right, Peter?" she asked, rapidly blinking as she gestured toward the door with her head.

"I could stay half an hour longer and play Avengers with the boys. If it's okay with you, Carrie."

"Oh, please, Mom? Please, please, please?" the boys asked, clasping their hands as they stared up at her with excitement.

Carrie glowered at him, communicating without words the extra-late bedtime would make tomorrow morning impossible. Still, he could see her struggling to say no. Capitulating, she nodded. "Okay, thirty minutes," she warned, holding up a finger. "After that, we're brushing teeth and straight to bed. Deal?"

"Deal!" they both shouted, running over to Peter and each grabbing a hand. They dragged him to sit on the floor between them and booted up the game. Charlie handed him a controller and detailed him on the functionality.

"You go first," Peter said. "Show me how it's done."

Charlie took the controller and began to play while Peter glanced at Sebastian. "He's really good at this level," Sebastian said.

Staring into the boy's eyes, Peter was overwhelmed with an onslaught of feelings which he struggled to contain. Sorrow at the time he'd lost. Anger at Carrie for keeping the secret. Rage at himself for forcing her to think he'd never accept their child. And love. Deep, abiding love filled his heart as the boy stared up at him with his blue-green eyes, a perfect amalgamation of his and Carrie's.

"I bet you're good at it too," he said, rubbing his son's hair as he nodded.

"I'm okay but I'm better at the next level. I like Hulk the best."

"Awesome. Can't wait for you to show me."

Looking over his shoulder, he glanced at Carrie and Ashlyn, arms around each other's waists as tears streamed down their faces. Realizing Carrie had probably told Scott, leading to tonight's babysitting duties, he understood Ashlyn knew their secret as well. In a town as small as Ardor Creek, everyone would know by tomorrow.

Turning back, he settled in with the boys, understanding his life had taken a drastic turn. Glowing in the luster of their crooked smiles, Peter didn't mind one damn bit. Actually, he was lucky as hell. Determined to embrace this new path, he placed his arms around their small shoulders and held on tight.

Chapter 9

Peter drove down the highway on Monday morning and glanced at Carrie in the passenger seat. Fingers fidgeted in her lap as she stared absently out the window.

"It's going to be fine," he said, reaching over and lacing their fingers. "We'll get all the information today."

"I know," she said, giving a soft smile. "I think I just want to get confirmation that you're a viable donor and I'll feel better."

"I treated my body like shit for years but I've been healthy as a horse for three years now. Hopefully, I'll be a candidate."

Those gorgeous eyes searched his before he focused back on the road. There were a lot of unspoken words between them since their tryst on the couch Thursday but they hadn't found time to discuss them. When you had two rambunctious boys in your life, finding private time was difficult. Once they figured out the medical plan, he would sit down with Carrie and discuss the multitude of topics they needed to hash out. Most importantly, Peter wanted to tell Sebastian he was his father. It would have to be done with caution and care, and he knew Carrie would guide him. She was such a great mom and always knew the right thing to say concerning her sons. Awed by her, he squeezed her hand.

She smiled, clenching him back as they turned down the street that led to Dr. Stevens' office. Once inside, they waited for a few minutes before a nurse led them down the hallway and directed them toward leather seats before a large desk. A man entered with salt-and-peppered hair and a warm smile.

"Hi, Carrie, nice to see you again," he said, shaking her hand. "And you must be the father."

"Peter Stratford," he said, noting the kind sparkle in the man's eyes. "Nice to meet you, Dr. Stevens."

"A pleasure," he said, sitting behind his desk and opening a manilla file. "So, Carrie tells me you're ready to donate a kidney."

"I am," Peter said with a nod. "As long as everything is okay. I...well, I was an addict for a long time, Dr. Stevens. I still am, of course, but I've been sober for almost three years. I hope I didn't permanently damage my kidneys in the process."

"Drug and alcohol abuse can sometimes preclude someone from donating but I looked over the diagnostic tests you sent me from the clinic near Ardor Creek and everything looks perfectly normal, Peter. As discussed, we're going to run a gamut of tests while you're here today but I don't foresee an issue with you donating a kidney to Sebastian."

"Thank god," Carrie whispered.

"The next steps are pretty well defined," Dr. Stevens said, sitting back in his chair. "As long as Peter's tests today check out, we'll schedule the transplant surgery for the second week of May. That's also dependent on our transplant social worker signing off as well, Peter. She'll evaluate you after your physical tests today to ensure you're mentally prepared for the surgery."

"I've had a lot of counseling since I got sober, Doc, and I'm fine with that. One concern I have is the administration of anesthesia. Is there a higher risk I could relapse from the effects?"

"That's a very good question. Our anesthesiologist, Dr. Crowley, is an expert at administering anesthesia to all types of patients. He has a specific protocol he follows with addicts and studies show that anesthesia has no statistically significant effect on relapse of any kind, whether it be drugs or alcohol. Dr. Crowley is part of our transplant team and he will discuss the regimen with you in our meetings."

"Okay," Peter said, looking relieved. "Sounds like you've done this a time or two, Dr. Stevens."

"A bit more than that but, yes, we've seen it all around here. Our team creates a detailed plan with each and every patient," Dr.

Stevens said with a nod. "In Sebastian's case, all of his evaluations were completed last week and he's been cleared to move forward. During the procedure, our team will remove Peter's right kidney and transplant it into Sebastian's vacant spot. We'll leave Sebastian's left kidney for now. Native kidneys with less function are fine in the body as long as they aren't causing any pain. If that kidney develops PKD down the road, we could always remove it but, hopefully, with the addition of Peter's healthy kidney, Sebastian's body will function normally."

"Will he still be able to play and do everything he can now?"

"Yes, with some limited restrictions. Peter's kidney should last him decades if we're lucky. When Sebastian's older, he'll possibly have to get another transplant. But, hopefully, we'll know well in advance and be able to put him on the donor list with plenty of time to spare."

"Okay," she whispered, covering her mouth. "I just wish he didn't have to go through any of this. I want him to be healthy."

"He can still lead an exceptionally healthy life as long as he eats well and gets plenty of exercise."

"Her boys have energy to spare," Peter said, "so exercise is definitely not a problem."

"That's good," Dr. Stevens said, grinning. "Some parents plop their kids in front of the TV and they don't ever get outside. That leads to high childhood obesity and diabetes rates. Fresh air and exercise are always good for kids."

"They love sports. I can barely get them off the soccer field half the time."

"That's fantastic. I can sense what a great mother you are, Carrie. You glow every time you speak about your sons."

"She's amazing," Peter said, reaching over and squeezing her hand.

"I try but I definitely fail a lot. It's the hardest job I've ever had, that's for sure."

"My wife tells me every day. I love being a father but she does most of the heavy lifting. Now that our kids are grown, she's begging them for grandbabies. The cycle never ends."

"So true," Carrie said with a laugh.

Settling back into the medical discussion, Dr. Stevens said, "Peter, your hospital stay will be three days to one week, depending on how quickly you recover. Upon release, you'll need to rest a lot for the first two weeks and will be fully healed in four to six weeks. Sebastian will need up to ten days' recovery in the hospital, although he could be released sooner if he heals quickly."

"As I discussed with your evaluation team last week, I have an extremely understanding boss and can perform my executive assistant functions from home. I'm prepared to take care of both of them once they're released."

"Excellent," Dr. Stevens said. "The new kidney will be a stranger to Sebastian's body so he'll need to take immunosuppressants to make sure his immune system doesn't reject the donated kidney. He'll take them as long as he has the kidney but the side effects can be managed and shouldn't overtly affect his daily functions. Since the drugs will weaken his immune system, the healthy diet and exercise are important."

"And I'll function fine with the kidney I have left?" Peter asked.

"Absolutely. The body only needs one but we're born with two. Pretty fortuitous in situations like this."

"Peter agreed to donate right away," Carrie said, gazing at him with more affection than he'd seen in years. "I'm so thankful for him."

"You're doing a good thing, Peter. It will help Sebastian live a long, healthy life."

"I'd do anything to help my son," Peter said, lifting Carrie's hand and kissing it. "And to help Carrie. She was my high school sweetheart, Dr. Stevens."

"Well, how lovely," he said, grinning. "Do either of you have any more questions before we get started on Peter's evaluation?"

"No, but I'm sure I'll have a million once we leave."

"That's perfectly fine, Carrie. You can call me anytime."

"Thank you."

"Okay, Peter, ready to get poked and prodded a bit?"

Standing, Peter gave a nod. "Ready, Doc. Let's do it. As long as there's no anal probe, I'm in."

"Oh my god," Carrie said, resting her head on her hand. "Peter!"

"A strong sense of humor always helps with recovery so you're already on your way, Peter," Dr. Stevens said, standing. "And I'll cancel the anal probe, no problem."

"See?" Peter asked in mock exasperation. "Good thing I asked."

"I promise he knows how to act like a normal human, Dr. Stevens. He always thinks he's funnier than he is."

"I'm hilarious, woman," he said, pulling her to stand and playfully scrunching his features.

"Come on, Peter," Dr. Stevens said, leading him from the office. "We can exchange jokes on our walk down the hallway. Carrie, you can sit in the waiting room while we do the damage. It will be several hours. There's a café in the lobby if you get bored."

Giving her a wink, Peter noticed her cheeks blush, causing his muscles to tense. She was so stunning under the staid fluorescent office lighting, he yearned to drag her into his arms and devour those pink lips. Since they were in public, he followed the kind doctor instead, ready to help his son.

C arrie scribbled in the notebook as Peter drove them home. He could almost see steam puffing from her ears as she made copious notes.

"Since the surgery is May twelfth, we'll get a hotel room in Scranton the night of May eleventh so we can get to the hospital early. Ashlyn and Scott have already agreed to watch Charlie, which is amazing. I need to do something really special for them." Lifting the pen to her teeth, she chewed on it as she contemplated. Lowering the pen, she resumed scribbling.

"We'll have them drive Charlie down on Sunday after the surgery so he can see Sebastian. He should be ready to see visitors by then. They can come in the early afternoon so they can get him home with plenty of time to spare so he's prepared for school that week."

Glancing at him, she pondered. "As discussed, you'll move into our guest bedroom so I can take care of you and Sebastian while you heal."

Peter grinned, loving her flushed cheeks as the thoughts buzzed in her brain.

"What? You're giving me a look."

"I just never thought we'd get to the point where you ask me to move in with you and I'd say yes. It only took us four decades."

"You can move in until you're well," she said, using the same stern tone she used with the boys. "After that, I'm shipping you back home."

The words hurt and Peter inhaled from the sting. He'd learned breathing techniques in rehab and now channeled his hurt and anger much more effectively. "So, you're still going to hate me even after donating a kidney? Low blow, Care Bear."

"Don't be ridiculous," she said, rolling her eyes. "Of course, I don't hate you. I'm beyond grateful for what you're doing for Sebastian. But it doesn't change our history, Peter."

Shooting her a look, his brow furrowed. "And what about the fact we almost set your couch on fire on Thursday night? Does that mean anything?"

"Attraction has never been our problem."

Peter's hands gripped the wheel as he realized she might never truly forgive him. Although he knew deep inside she loved him as he so vehemently loved her, it was possible Carrie would never open her heart to him again. Perhaps no amount of love could erase transgressions that ran so deep. Still, he felt a door had been opened when they made love, if only slightly, and if there was even a sliver of a chance he could win her love one last time, he was determined to try like hell. It would take time and patience, but he was finally ready to give her everything. Hopefully, her tender heart would receive it.

"Well, I'll take whatever scraps you throw me," he said, thrilled at the offer to move in during his recovery. "I'll take the guest bedroom and maybe you can dress up in one of those sexy nurse uniforms and take my temperature." He waggled his brows.

"You wish," she muttered, training her attention back on the notebook. Fuck yeah, he wished. It might be the sexiest wish he'd ever conjured.

"I'm wondering how to explain everything to the boys," she said, eyes narrowing as she stared out the window. "I think we just need to sit them down tonight and explain everything as gently and straightforward as possible."

"Okay," he said, heartbeat accelerating at the thought of telling Sebastian he was his father. "I'll be right by your side, honey. We'll answer all their questions together."

"I'm glad you'll be doing the surgery along with him," she said, sliding her hand over his forearm and squeezing. "It will make it cool and much less scary, I think. They do love their Uncle Peter. For someone who didn't want kids, you're pretty great with them."

"I was never against kids, Carrie," he said, frustrated she always saw everything in black and white. "Kids and family represented roots, and I didn't want to be tied to Ardor Creek."

"But now you're stuck with us." Her expression was sad.

"That's what you don't get. I see things differently now. Hell, I'll be forty soon. People are capable of changing their perspective, you know?"

"I'm not sure people really change that much," she said, shrugging. "Maybe it's hard for me to understand because I always knew what I wanted. I'm still the same person and probably always will be."

"Well, I love the person you are so I hope you never change."

Her gaze trailed to her lap and he ached to say more, but the energy between them had grown heavy so he decided to change the subject.

"I can't wait to tell Sebastian I'm his dad. I'm also scared shitless."

Turning her head against the leather seat, she smiled. "You'll be fine. Like I said, they love you. Let's grab pizza and we'll eat in the living room while we talk. Kara picked them up from school today and they should be home now."

"Want to call in the order?"

"Sure," she said, lifting her phone.

Filled with anxious excitement, Peter drove them home to Ardor Creek.

Chapter 10

♥

Carrie sat with her boys on the carpeted floor as they ate pizza with Peter while the TV softly droned in the background. Eventually, they devoured the two pies and Carrie walked over to switch off the TV. Sitting back down, she stared at three men in her life, hoping she didn't fail as she broke the news.

"I want to talk to you both about something that has to do with Uncle Peter."

"Okay," they both said, rapt with attention.

"You know that Mom has been friends with Peter since we were younger than Charlie, right?"

They both nodded and Carrie felt Peter slide his hand into hers. Smiling, she squeezed. "When moms and dads care about each other, they hold each other really tight and sometimes that makes a baby."

"The man rubs his penis on the woman's vagina," Sebastian blurted-ed.

Carrie's eyes almost bugged from her head. "Where did you hear that, young man?"

Shrugging, he said, "Chris Laredo told us at recess last month, Mom. Everybody knows."

Reeling from his words, Carrie looked at Peter, who lifted his shoulder.

"I mean, he's not wrong."

"You're not helping," she whispered. Turning to her boys, she noticed Charlie staring at his crotch as if trying to figure out his brother's words.

"We'll have a separate discussion on how babies are made later," she said in her stern mommy tone. "For now, I'm going to tell you something really cool. Well, I hope you'll think it's cool."

They both waited in anticipation.

Inhaling, Carrie said, "Peter and I held each other really tight before Sebastian was born and we ended up making him together." Her gaze darted between the kids, judging their reaction. "Peter is your biological father, Sebastian."

"What's bi-lodge-cal?" Charlie asked.

"It means Sebastian has traits and genes from both me and Peter, like his light hair and the blue in his eyes, just like you have your dad's brown hair and brown eyes."

"I hate my dad," Charlie said, frowning. "Can Peter be my bi-lodge-cal dad too?"

"We don't hate anyone in this home," Carrie said, although she hated Jeff with a passion too. "What did grandpa always say?"

"You can always find love in your heart for everyone," the boys uttered in unison.

"That's right."

"I'm proud to be your dad, Sebastian, and I care about both of you very much. Biology doesn't really matter when you care about someone. Right, Carrie?"

"That's right," she said, noticing how quiet Sebastian was. "Honey, what do you think about this? Any feelings you have are perfectly fine and you can tell us."

Sebastian studied Peter, gaze roving over his frame, before pursing his lips. "It's pretty cool, I guess. I really like hanging out with Uncle Peter. He's pretty good at video games and soccer."

Peter smiled. "You two are way better than me but I like playing with you."

Sebastian scratched his arm, appearing as if he wanted to say more.

"What is it, sweetie?" Carrie asked. "You can tell us how you're feeling."

"Do I have to call you 'Dad' now? Are you going to marry Mom and live with us?"

"We're going to have a lot of changes over the next few weeks and months, and I want to discuss those with you too. But you don't have to call Peter 'Dad' or anything else that doesn't feel natural. It's up to you."

"You can still call me 'Uncle Peter,'" he said. "I love it when you guys call me that."

"Okay," Sebastian said, nodding.

"And we're not getting married but I do have some news about Peter living with us for a while. It has to do with the pain Sebastian has been having recently and how we're going to fix it."

"His pee is red," Charlie said. "He showed me."

"I know, sweetie," she said, reaching over and smoothing his hair. "Your brother is sick and we want to make him better."

"How?" Sebastian asked.

Pulling out the book she'd placed under the coffee table, she opened it to the page that showed an anatomical drawing of a body with the organs labeled.

"This is our body," she said, circling her finger over the picture. "Here's the heart and the legs and the head. See?"

The boys nodded.

"These organs are called kidneys. There are two of them and they sit on your sides, right here." She pointed to her own side and the boys examined their bodies, pointing as well. "Yep, you've both got it."

"Man, you both are smart. I didn't understand anatomy until I learned it from your mom when I was a teenager."

She sent Peter a scathing look, although it melted away at his sultry wink.

"Anyway," she said, rolling her eyes before focusing on the boys. "The kidneys are like a sponge that sucks away waste in the body and then it comes out when you pee."

"Ew," Sebastian said, wrinkling his nose.

"I know," she said, grinning. "It sounds gross but your kidneys need to function properly so they can cleanse your body of the bad stuff. Unfortunately, Sebastian's aren't working very well and we've decided to get him a new one."

"How?" Sebastian asked.

"Well, Sebastian, since I'm your biological father and you have my genes, I can give you one of my kidneys. It will help you feel a lot better than the one you have right now."

Sebastian pondered. "Will it make the red pee and my stomach aches go away?"

"Yes, sweetie," Carrie said.

"I'd really like that. It hurts a lot."

"I know, baby," she said, setting the book on the table and scooching to sit between them. Pulling Sebastian into her lap, she kissed his head. "Uncle Peter is going to donate his kidney to you so you don't hurt anymore."

"I want a kidney too," Charlie said, pouting.

"I only have one to spare, kid, or I swear I'd give you one too."

"Let's be thankful you're not sick too, buddy," Carrie said, drawing him on her lap, balancing her boys on both thighs even though they were too big to fit. She didn't give a damn. Holding them while Peter gazed upon them with affection made her heart swell. "I need you to help me while Sebastian and Uncle Peter recover from their surgery, Charlie. I hope you don't mind. It's a really important job and I need a really smart and strong helper."

"I'll help you, Mom," Charlie said. His crooked smile spurred tears that burned her eyes.

"Thank you, baby. I love you both so much." She gave them each wet kisses before they slithered off her lap.

"Is Uncle Peter going to live here after he gives me the kidney?" Sebastian asked.

"For a while," she said, running her fingers through his tawny hair. "Until he feels better. Charlie and I are going to help you both recover. It will take several weeks and you'll have to rest in bed a lot."

"When I'm better can I play soccer again?"

"Absolutely. The surgery will help you play soccer even better because your body won't hurt anymore."

"That's cool."

"It is pretty cool," Peter said.

"Thank you for helping me, Uncle Peter," Sebastian said. "I'm glad I have your genes."

"Me too, kid," Peter said as Carrie noticed tears well in his eyes. "I'm really glad. I care about all of you a whole lot."

"We care about you too, right boys?"

They nodded and Carrie expelled a ragged breath, taken by the poignant moment. Drawing the kids back into her sides, she gazed at Peter, wondering how in the hell they'd ended up here...and contemplating why it felt so damn perfect. Nothing with Peter had ever been perfect. Instead, it had been heart-wrenching and extremely painful. Rocking with her boys in her arms, she wondered if, finally, after all this time, their luck had ultimately changed.

Chapter 11

♥

That evening, once the boys were in bed, Carrie and Peter sat on the front porch in comfortable silence, weighing the gravity of the turns their lives had taken.

"They both took the news fine," Peter said, gently rocking in the wooden chair. "About me being Sebastian's dad and about the upcoming surgery."

"I'm not sure they really understand either revelation," she said, staring at the star-filled sky, "but that's okay. I'll need to check in on them a lot and ask how they're feeling."

"We'll need to check in on them," he said, grasping her hand. "I want to be here for you and for them."

Her eyes darted between his. "For how long?" she whispered.

He gave her the same grin that had all but melted her panties when she was seventeen. "Forever sounds pretty good."

Rolling her eyes, she drew away her hand. "I don't believe in forever anymore."

Sighing, he rested his head against the broad back of the chair. "That's my fault, I guess. Like so many other things. I wish there was a way to tell you how sorry I was."

"Well, you could say it."

Carrie wondered how his head didn't snap off when he jerked to look at her. "Say what?"

Smiling at how daft he was, she leaned forward. "You could say, 'I'm sorry', Peter. You rarely have. Words mean something, you know."

"I feel like I've apologized a thousand times," he said, appearing baffled.

"Sure, you've said you hated yourself for leaving and you apologized for being terrible to me as part of your sobriety apology, but you rarely look me in the eye and say those two simple little words."

"Wow," he said, running his hand over his face. "Am I really that much of an idiot?"

"Yeah, you are, but you're too much a part of my life to write off," she teased.

"Especially now."

"Especially now," she said with a nod.

"Carrie Elizabeth Longwood," he said, rotating to face her and grasping her hand. "I'm so damn sorry. For everything."

Wrinkling her nose, she said, "You went all out with the middle name."

Chuckling, he squeezed her hand. "I had to make it formal. A true apology. For being so awful and for leaving you so many times."

"Thank you," she said, swiping away the errant tear that trailed down her cheek. "I'm sorry for not telling you about Sebastian. You've been pretty great at not castigating me for it."

"If he wasn't sick, I'd probably be more pissed, but circumstances like this put everything in perspective. Life's too short to waste it being angry. I learned that in rehab."

"It is," she said wistfully, gazing at their joined hands.

"Could we try one more time, Care Bear? I want to so badly."

Inhaling, she pondered. "I think there's a point where you squander all your second chances, Peter."

"Carrie—"

"Wait," she interrupted, holding up her free hand. "Just let me finish."

He looked so contrite, like a scolded puppy as he nodded, and her heart swelled with the emotion she'd only ever felt for him.

"I don't think I'd survive it, Peter. If I let you into my world and you left me again. It might shatter every last shred holding my heart together. If it was just me, it would be so much easier to consider, but I have the boys now and I can't be a mom to them if I'm a wreck inside."

"What if I promised—?"

"You're awesome at promises, Peter. You're just really bad at keeping them."

His lips curved into a sad smile. "I always have been. You're right about that."

Carrie rubbed the smooth skin of his hand, unable to stop the gentle caress. Touching him had always come so easily to her and she reveled in their tender grasp.

"What if we took it day by day?" he finally asked, gazing at her with those clear blue eyes. "No promises and no labels. Just you and me and the boys, testing things out and seeing how we all fit together."

Arching a brow, she asked, "I assume that means you want us to fit together between the sheets too?"

Hissing out a breath, he clenched her hand. "Fuck yes. I can't stop thinking about making love to you, Carrie. You woke the beast on that couch the other night. I remembered how amazing it was to be with you and I want more. Everything you'll give me. Every hour of the damn day—"

"Okay," she said, rolling her eyes. "I get it. You want to bang me senseless."

"And you want to bang me too," he said, waggling his brows. "Don't even try to lie to me, honey."

Biting her lip, she contemplated him under the moonlight.

"What is it?"

"I just..." tugging her hand away, she gestured between them. "You've been with a lot of other women and I've only been with you, Jeff and Brandon," she said, referencing the man she'd dated in her mid-twenties. "I feel kind of weird about it. Like, maybe you discovered some exciting sexual escapades in the city I've never heard of."

Blowing a breath through puffed cheeks, he rubbed his forehead. "Well, this is awkward but I guess we need to have this discussion so we can get everything out in the open and move the hell on."

"Look, I'm confident and have really grown into myself. I think I could probably put up a Tinder profile and get laid pretty easily. I'm not the lovelorn girl you left behind all those years ago. Maybe I need to even out the tally and sleep with some other men before we knock boots again."

"I'm not sure how we skipped to you fucking someone else but it will be a cold day in hell before anyone else touches you."

Scoffing, she waved her hand. "You have no claim over me. You gave that up years ago."

"Well, I'm taking it back," he said, standing and tugging her to her feet. "No one else, Carrie. I mean it." Thrusting his fingers into the hair at her nape, he stared into her eyes.

"No one else for you either," she almost whispered.

"Never again," he said, inching closer. "I only want you."

Heavy breaths mingled as they both stood firm.

"It wasn't what you think," he said softly, stroking her cheeks with his thumbs. "I was coked out and drunk most of the time. I was never serious about any of the women I was with. Hell, half of them were high-end escorts my work buddies and I bought with all the money we threw away."

"Well, that makes me feel great since we barebacked the other night," she mumbled.

"I always carried condoms and was adamant about that, at least."

"The women and the drugs reinforce that I was never enough for you. You always wanted something more exciting."

"I wanted to escape my unhappiness and my abuse. I was so sure if I left Ardor Creek, I'd leave it behind for good. It took me several brushes with death to realize I'll always carry it inside. Now, I've learned to manage it but it's hard, Carrie. My AA and NA sponsors are great but it really comes down to my own self-reflection and inner strength."

"I'm so proud of your sobriety, Peter," she said, feeling her eyes well with tears. "I wish I'd been able to help you more."

"There was nothing you could've done. It was my path to take. But nothing was ever more important to me than you, even when I was drowning. I thought about you all the time, honey. I always have." The soft breeze trailed over them and he tucked a wayward curl behind her ear. "I never thought I'd earn the chance to make love to you again but you rocked my world the other night. I haven't been with anyone since rehab and I get a shit ton of checkups. I'm clean but if you want to use protection, I will. I want you to feel safe with me."

Contemplating him, she cupped his face. "I believe you. On that, at least."

"But not on other things?"

"I don't understand why you want to try again. You're stuck in Ardor Creek and you're lonely. I think I'm just a fallback now that your mom is gone. The time will come when you want to move back to the city."

"No," he said, closing the distance and aligning their bodies. "I'm here for the long haul. The city represents the version of myself that was toxic and broken. And as far as being a fallback," he leaned closer, gazing into her soul, "that's just fucking ridiculous. You're the one, Carrie. You always have been. I'm just old enough and wise enough to finally accept it."

Unable to process the poignant words, she pursed her lips. "You're definitely old. The jury's out on wise."

Breathing a laugh, he nuzzled her nose with his. "True. But I try to learn every day. Let me try with you, honey. Maybe this time we'll actually get it right."

Sliding her arms around his neck, she let the smile break free. "I'm not sure the universe is ready to accept us as anything but tortured, star-crossed lovers."

"Fuck the universe," he said, resting his forehead against hers. "We'll show it who's boss."

Elation coursed through her body at his warm embrace and their easy comradery. "Okay. I like the sound of day by day."

"Yeah?" Excitement laced his handsome features.

Nodding, she bit her lip. "No labels or terms. We'll just go with the flow. You should probably go ahead and move in now so the boys can get used to you being here for the week and a half before the surgery."

"And so we can bang?"

"If you're a good boy."

"Is it weird that I get turned on when you use that stern mommy tone with me?"

Laughing, she nodded. "Probably."

"I don't care," he said, sliding his hands to her ass and squeezing. "It's so fucking sexy."

Wetness gushed from her core at his silken words. "Peter—"

His lips crushed hers, sucking away the word as his tongue impaled her mouth. Groaning, she pulled him close, her body humming as it always did when he held her. Thrusting her fingers into his thick hair, their tongues slid together until her muscles turned to jelly.

"I think it's time I showed you the guest room," she murmured against his lips.

"Fuck yes," he said, crouching and lifting her. Yelping, she wrapped her legs around his waist.

"Peter!" she hissed, not wanting to wake the boys as they slept upstairs. "We have to be quiet."

"Oh, I'll be quiet, honey," he said, carrying her across the porch and through the front door before softly closing it behind them. Trailing to the guest bedroom, he clicked the door closed and collapsed on the queen-sized bed. Running his fingers over her cheek, he grinned as a shaft of moonlight from the nearby window illuminated his features. "I can be really quiet when my mouth is buried in your sweet pussy."

Shuddering, she wrapped her arms around his neck and pressed her lips to his. "Show me how quiet you can be."

"Now you're using the stern tone on purpose."

"Maybe," she said, pushing his head lower. "Take off my pants and show me it's working."

Complying, he proceeded to show her how skilled his mouth could be even when silent, although it was quite difficult for Carrie to contain her satisfied groans in the darkened house.

Chapter 12

Peter set out to prepare himself for the surgery and following weeks of recovery. He reached out to his accounting clients and informed them he would be taking a leave of absence until at least early July. Thankfully, there was another accountant in town, Jennifer Rodgers, whom Peter had known since childhood, and she agreed to handle any overflow or customer questions while he was out of commission.

Peter also went through Scott's ledgers at Grillo Design and Construction, ensuring everything was in order with the firm's various jobs and contracts before he entered the hospital. Scott had given Peter ten percent of GDC in exchange for running the financial end, showcasing his friend's generous heart. Since Scott detested all things financial and relished the construction side, it worked out perfectly.

In fact, Peter thought as he packed the suitcase atop his bed in preparation to stay at Carrie's house, things had worked out pretty well for him since returning to Ardor Creek three years ago. He'd come home broken and weary after being arrested and waking up in the back of a police cruiser on the way to jail. Once they booked him and threw him in the cell, two of the other detainees had beat him senseless while the guard looked on, silent and stoic. In that moment, as his face was getting pounded in, Peter had seen flashes of his father's fists as they'd landed blows on him and his mother years ago. Vowing to end the violence and destruction in his life, he'd left his fancy Wall Street job, sold his penthouse condo, and returned home to Ardor Creek.

His mother, Doris, had been elated to have him home. Her health was failing and Peter knew he only had a few years left with her. After completing a month-long rehab in a facility outside Scranton, he'd sought out local Alcoholics Anonymous and Narcotics Anonymous meetings, determined to live a sober life. Although he would always be an addict, he understood he had the power to choose to be sober. To choose his own destiny.

There were times when the addict inside flared so vehemently, Peter would clench his fingers, trying to conjure the feel of a tumbler in his hand, full of scotch or tequila. One large gulp and the pain and yearning would all but disappear. But the relief would be temporary and one sip would open the door to more alcohol, illicit drugs, and the loss of control. Furthermore, it would dredge up all the self-loathing Peter tried so hard to contain with therapy and council from his sponsors.

Now, three years later, he felt a sense of peace and calm he hadn't felt in so long. Brow furrowing as he stood beside his bed, he tried to remember ever feeling so centered. It was revelatory to someone who'd come so close to hitting rock bottom, never to return.

His phone chimed atop the bedside table and Peter grinned at the Caller ID.

"Hey, hon," he said, putting the phone on speaker as he continued to pack.

"Hey," Carrie's sweet voice called. "Did you get everything packed?"

"Almost done. I should be over there in half an hour."

"Okay, we'll have dinner and spend some time with the boys before they go to bed."

"Sounds good. I also want to ask you something."

"Sure."

Inhaling a deep breath, Peter felt the nerves settle in. "I want to spend some time with Sebastian before the surgery. I know it's only a week away but I thought maybe we could hang this weekend, just the two of us."

"I think that's a lovely idea. Charlie has a soccer game on Saturday at ten a.m. Why don't I take him to the game and spend the day with him while you and Sebastian hang out?"

"I'd like that," Peter said, feeling his eyebrows draw together. "I was thinking of taking him to the Claws 'N' Paws zoo. It's about an hour away and has all sorts of animals and hiking trails. Would he enjoy something like that? I have no idea what a ten-year-old kid enjoys."

"I think he'd love it. Honestly, anything you do with him is fine because he looks up to you, but the zoo sounds perfect."

Sitting on the side of the bed, Peter took the phone off speaker and lifted it to his ear. "A part of me is terrified of letting them down, Carrie. My old man was such a shitty father and I'm always one drink away from fucking everything up. I want to promise you I won't fail at this but I have no idea if I can."

"Well, at least you're not making false promises anymore," she said, a teasing lilt in her voice. "We're making progress."

"I told you, honey, I'm ready to try. I just hope I don't let you guys down. One of the reasons I didn't pursue you when I came home and your divorce was finalized was because I wasn't sure you wanted a junkie as a role model for the boys."

"We all make mistakes, Peter. Humans are messy and flawed. But forgiveness is a powerful gift and so is self-reflection. You've gotten pretty good at that and I have faith you can do this."

"That I can be Sebastian's father?"

"Yes. You're going to be awesome. You already are."

Deliberating, he ran his fingers over the soft comforter. "I wonder how I'd fare at being a husband." Silence stretched through the phone as the air grew heavy. "Maybe if I stay on this path, we can eventually find out."

"Day by day, Peter," she said. "Let's get through the surgery and the recovery and see how things go."

"Okay," he said, nodding. "Sometimes I wonder why you chose me all those years ago, Carrie. You followed me after that stupid dodgeball game and I fell for you like a damn rock. But I often berate myself for never earning your affection. We just jumped in headfirst. If we do make it to the finish line, I'm going to sweep you off your feet like you deserve. I just need to make sure you won't reject me and smash my heart when we get there."

The air seemed to crackle through the phone. "I'm not the one who's done the heart smashing in this relationship, Peter."

"True, but we're definitely on more even ground now that I know about Sebastian."

Carrie sighed. "Yes. We're both capable of hurting each other terribly. Does it really need pointing out?"

"Yes, because I want it to change. I don't ever want to hurt you again."

"Then don't," she almost whispered.

"You either," he whispered back.

"I won't. I'm so grateful for what you're doing for Sebastian. Thank you, Peter."

Contemplating, he stared at the suitcase. Finally, he said, "I'm doing it for Sebastian but I'm also doing it for you. You know that, right?"

"Yes."

Standing, he trailed to the bathroom to find his toiletry bag. "Well, then, we should probably get on with it. Like I said, I'll be over soon. What's for dinner?"

"Lasagna and Greek salad."

"Yum. I like the idea of you cooking for me and us playing house. Maybe you can feed me some leftovers while only wearing a cute little apron later?"

"Don't push it, buddy," she muttered, causing him to chuckle. "You have some weird fantasies."

"About you? I have a million of them, honey. I'm still imagining you in the sexy nurse uniform. That's been on a constant loop in my brain ever since I brought it up."

"Well, you're going to get 'functional mom who needs to cook dinner for her boys' instead, sorry."

"As long as you use the stern mommy tone, I'm one-hundred percent okay with that—"

"Goodbye, Peter," she droned.

"Bye, hon. See you in a bit."

"See you soon."

Clicking off the phone, Peter couldn't contain his smile. Excited for the weeks and months ahead with Carrie and the kids, he finished packing so he could continue on the path of becoming the man he was ready to be.

Peter had a fantastic time with Sebastian at the zoo although he was exhausted by the end of the day. Even though the kid was about to have major surgery for a bum kidney, he had a plethora of energy. Carrie was managing his pain with Children's Tylenol until the surgery and he appeared fine, although Peter kept an eye out for any noticeable symptoms. Thankfully, the kid just plowed on, enthralled by the animals—most notably, the tigers and lions. After seeing the various wildlife, they decided to check out the walking trails that snaked throughout the property. As they hiked along the last trail they'd designated for the day, Peter marveled at his son's infectious and questioning nature.

"I can't believe Mom was that good at softball," Sebastian said as they walked along the dirt path. "She never plays wiffleball with us in the backyard."

"She was awesome, kid, and really good at soccer too."

"Yeah, she plays soccer with us sometimes. So does Ashlyn. They're both pretty good."

"What about Scott? I thought he played with you guys?"

"He's okay," he said, shrugging. "But Ashlyn's better."

"Oh, man," Peter said, chuckling. "Can't wait to pass that along."

Leaning down, Sebastian picked up a rock. "Want to skip it on the lake over there?"

"Sure." They ambled to the small body of water and Peter marveled at the boy's skilled toss. "Nice job. Who taught you how to do that?"

"My dad," he mumbled.

"Do you miss seeing your dad?" Peter asked, bending down and locating his own rock to toss as he anticipated the answer.

"Not really. He was pretty mean to us and Mom. He yelled a lot and hit Charlie really hard one time. He used to grab my arm and pull me across the yard when I wouldn't come inside and brush my teeth. I tried not to cry because crying's stupid, but sometimes I did when I went to my room."

"That's okay," Peter said, watching the stone skip across the water. "My dad was rough with me when I was your age and I used to cry too, even though I didn't want to."

"You did?" Green-blue eyes gazed up at him, and Peter ran his hand over the boy's hair.

"Yeah. Crying's not that bad and sometimes it makes you feel better."

"Mom would cry a lot once we went to bed. Dad would be sleeping and she would come downstairs and sit on the couch. I snuck out of my room and could hear her from the top of the stairs."

Regret swamped Peter as he digested his son's words. "I'm really sorry to hear that."

Nodding, he picked up another rock and skipped it. "She was always fine in the morning, though, and I don't think she knew I saw her. Don't say anything, okay?"

"Not a word, buddy."

"I don't really miss him and Mom says we might never see him again."

"Does that make you sad?"

"No. I like it better without him here. And it's really fun now that you're staying with us."

"I'm happy to hang out with you guys while we recover. We can compare our scars."

Sebastian beamed, causing Peter's heart to thump in his chest. "That will be cool."

Nodding, Peter threw one last stone across the river, marveling at Sebastian's wide eyes.

"Wow, that one went far."

"Yep." Wiping his hands on his pants, he smiled. "Ready to head back to the car?"

They walked in silence as the sun set low in the sky, and Peter wondered what was on the kid's mind. Finally, he lifted those questioning orbs and asked, "Are you going to marry my mom?"

"I don't know," he said, trying to be as honest as possible. "I've always cared about your mom a lot but it hasn't ever been the right time for us to get married."

"Maybe you can get married now."

"Would you like that?"

"Yeah. I don't think you'll make Mom cry like my dad did. She always smiles weird like this when she's on the phone with you." He gave a goofy grin. "I think she *loooooves* you."

"Well, that's nice to hear. I smile a lot when I talk to her too. Your mom's pretty special."

"Yeah. Sometimes I feel bad because I'm mean to Charlie and she gets mad at me. But he's so annoying sometimes," he said, rolling his eyes.

"Little brothers will always be annoying but you're lucky you have one. I was an only child and always wished I had a brother or sister."

"I guess. I feel bad when I'm mean to Charlie. Sometimes I can't help it."

Thinking of all the times Peter had treated Carrie terribly and felt awful afterward, he understood the sentiment. "Remorse sucks, kid. Trust me on that."

"What's remorse?"

"Feeling bad or really sorry for something."

Sebastian's lips flattened as he contemplated the new word.

"But you always apologize, right?"

"Yeah."

"That's what counts the most. I know Charlie loves you as much as you love him."

Eventually, they made it to the car and headed home under the blazing sunset. Once back at Carrie's house, Peter observed the boys settle in to play video games before dinner. Tugging Carrie's wrist, he pulled her through the back door onto the small patio.

"What's that smile for?" she asked, threading her arms around his neck.

"I think I had my first important father-son talk today and I didn't blow it."

"About what?"

"Just guy stuff. I'd tell you but I'd have to kill you." He winked. "I really enjoyed spending the day with him."

"Awesome. One serious talk down, a million to go. I'm probably going to solicit your help with that whole 'how babies are made' talk one day soon. If you think you can handle it."

He puffed out a breath. "That's a big leap but I can give it a go."

Chuckling, she placed a soft peck on his lips. "We'll figure it out together."

"It's so nice to see you smile like this, honey." Thinking of Sebastian's words, he vowed to do his best to ensure she never cried again.

"It is nice. The weeks ahead are going to be really intense but, for now, I feel pretty good."

"Good enough to sneak into the guest room tonight?"

Squeezing one eye shut, she studied him. "We'll see."

"I'll be waiting," he murmured before waggling his brows.

After dinner, they all eventually settled into bed and Peter lay wide awake on the soft sheets, anticipating her presence. Sure enough, the doorknob turned and she slipped inside dressed in cute little shorts and a tight tank top that showcased her pert nipples.

Gently closing the door, she slid in beside him. "We have to be quiet," she whispered.

"Okay," he said, loving how she slithered atop his body. Tugging her down for a kiss, he slid his hands to cup the mounds of her ass, pulling her into his straining erection. "How many organs can I donate for the chance to hold you like this every night?"

Breathing a laugh, she nuzzled his nose with hers. "Let's start with one and see where that takes us."

Pulling her shorts to the side, he gripped his shaft and slid the head over her wet opening, loving her resulting hiss.

"You're naked. Guess you were pretty sure of yourself."

"I always sleep naked, especially when there's a chance a sexy woman will sneak into my room."

Gazing deep into her eyes, he pushed into her tight warmth, feeling so connected to her as she whispered his name. The room was dark with soft shafts of moonlight filtering through the window. Gripping her ass, he held her in place as they slowly loved each other.

"So much for foreplay," she teased against his lips as her slick walls enveloped his aching cock.

"Sorry, honey," he said, sliding his fingers into her soft hair. "I'm going to be incapacitated for weeks and need to feel you."

"I'll take care of you," she murmured before capturing his lips with hers.

Plunging his tongue into her mouth, Peter closed his eyes, consumed with pleasure. Tight, wet folds slid around his engorged cock as he worked himself into her body. Wishing he could fuck her forever and never leave the intimate moment, he lifted his lids.

"Carrie..." he whispered.

The pace of her hips increased as she rode him, soft whimpers escaping her throat.

Feeling the insane urge to claim her—to ensure she remembered their passionate loving while he recovered—he flipped them over and pulled out, dragging the shorts off her legs before aligning the head of his shaft with her drenched entrance.

"Fuck me hard," she commanded.

"No," he whispered, sliding only the head of his cock inside as her eyes widened. "We're taking this one slow, honey. I want you to remember how good this feels."

Her breathy moan set him on fire and he began to slide into her quivering folds. Dragging his steel against her softness, he reveled in the desire that sparkled in her stunning eyes. "Yes, sweetheart. You're so fucking gorgeous."

Crimson hair dragged across the pillow as she writhed below him.

He moved his hips in the circular motion that caused his cock to stimulate the tiny bundle of nerves deep within. "There you are. I remember that spot."

"Peter..."

"Right fucking there," he said, clenching his teeth as her cheeks flushed in the moonlight. "Are you going to explode for me, honey?" Increasing the pace of his hips, he fucked her in the rhythm that drove her wild.

"*Ohmygod...*" she breathed, head tossing back on the pillow as her eyes clenched shut. A strangled moan leaped from her throat as her body began to shudder. Feeling his own release on the horizon, he rested his forehead against the pulsing vein at her neck.

Convulsions racked her body as the orgasm took hold, those sexy nails digging into his shoulders. Biting the soft skin of her neck, he moaned as his balls tightened. The wet tissues of her taut channel gripped him in a vice he never wanted to escape. Clutching her close, he set the climax free, shooting pulses of sticky release into her sweet body.

Growling like a possessive caveman, he emptied inside her, wanting to claim every inch and cover her in his essence. "Mine," he growled.

Soft, sated giggles enveloped them as she relaxed beneath him. "I'm pretty sure it's *mine.*"

Shuddering out the last drops of his release, he breathed in her scent as he tried to form words. "Mine," he repeated, unable to utter anything even remotely clever.

"Fine. I'll give you this one since you're giving up a kidney." Her nails trailed over his sweaty back. "You can officially claim my pussy as yours. Temporarily, of course."

"Fuck that," he muttered, kissing her soft skin. "Forever."

Her chest rose and fell beneath his cheek as they settled into sated silence. Sleep began to creep upon his languid frame and he felt her shift underneath.

"No," he murmured, clutching her close. "Stay."

"I can't," she said, placing a tender kiss on his temple. "I'm okay with sneaking down here but I need to sleep in my own bed. Sometimes the boys come into my room when they have a nightmare."

Feeling his lips form a pout, he tried to think of something that would convince her to stay.

"Good night, Peter," she said, gently extricating herself from his grasp as he mourned the loss of her soft skin. Giving him one final peck on the forehead, she slipped on her shorts and left the room.

Sighing, Peter snuggled into the mattress, holding the extra pillow tight, hating that it wasn't Carrie's sweet, warm body instead.

Chapter 13

♥

The week flew by and before Peter could blink, Thursday morning arrived. As he ate breakfast at the small round table in the kitchen, he observed the flurry of activity that comprised getting Charlie ready for school and his stay with Scott and Ashlyn.

"Everything is packed and I'll drop your suitcase off at Scott's office on our way to Scranton," Carrie said, crouching and cupping Charlie's cheek. "Do you have any more questions for me before we leave?"

Charlie shook his head and Carrie smiled. "Okay, buddy, hug your brother. Next time you see him, he'll have one of Peter's kidneys."

"I hope your surgery goes okay, Sebastian," Charlie said, approaching the table where his brother sat.

"Thanks," Sebastian muttered, taking a bite of his bagel.

"Sebastian David Lawrence, please stand up and give your brother a hug."

Rolling his eyes, Sebastian stood and hugged Charlie.

"I love you," Charlie said, squeezing.

Peter hid his grin as Carrie crossed her arms and tapped her foot. "What do you say, Sebastian?"

"I love you too," he murmured before releasing. Sitting back down, he took another bite of his bagel.

"Bye, Uncle Peter," Charlie said, enveloping him in a hug.

"Bye, buddy," he said, affection welling in his chest as he held tight. "Be good for Ashlyn and Scott."

"I forgot to pack Bear, Mom," Charlie said, disengaging and running out of the kitchen. "Be right back."

When he was gone, Carrie resumed packing the lunch on the counter. "You need to be nice to your brother, Sebastian," she scolded. "You're older and he looks up to you."

"I hugged him back, Mom, geez!"

"You're not going to see him for a while and remember what we said when Grandma passed away? You always wanted to hug her one more time and were never able to. That's why we should always seize the moment to tell someone we love them."

Sebastian seemed contrite as he stared at the table. Peter could almost see the wheels turning in his mind as he digested her words. When Charlie ran back into the kitchen with a stuffed bear, Sebastian stood and walked over. "I'll miss you while I'm in the hospital, Charlie," he said, hugging his brother.

Carrie gave a satisfied smile as she wrapped the sandwich in plastic wrap and set it in the lunchbox. Handing it to Charlie, she ruffled his hair. "You ready to go catch the bus?"

"Can you pack him?" he asked, holding up Bear.

"Sure thing." Grasping his hand, she set the stuffed animal on the counter and led Charlie out the front door, returning once the bus had safely picked him up.

"Okay, guys, we'll leave in thirty minutes. We have to be at the hospital by eleven for the pre-op tests and meetings."

They gathered up their suitcases and loaded into Carrie's SUV, Sebastian playing video games in the back seat as she drove.

"Are you nervous?" she asked.

"I don't know," he said, clutching the handle above the door. "I've had a few minor surgeries but nothing this intense. And nothing when I was this old."

Snickering, she nodded. "We certainly aren't spring chickens anymore. I'll take care of you, though."

"I know you will." Grasping her hand, he squeezed. "I'll try not to be a truculent patient."

"I'll believe it when I see it," she said, playfully scrunching her features.

They arrived at the hospital, and Peter and Sebastian were whisked away for pre-op tests. Once those were complete, they sat down to have one last meeting with the transplant team. Peter was definitely nervous but tamped down the anxiety, understanding he needed to be strong for Sebastian. If he was trepidatious, he could only imagine how scary the situation was for a ten-year-old.

Eventually, they settled into the hotel room with two double beds. They could only have a small meal before the early morning surgery and Carrie ordered them all salads. The food would hopefully help Sebastian digest the first dose of anti-rejection medicine, which he swallowed without complaint. Afterward, they video chatted with Charlie, Ashlyn, and Scott before prepping for bed. Once they were all in their PJs, Peter climbed into bed beside his son and they lay in the dark as the baseball game droned on TV.

"Are you scared, Uncle Peter?" he whispered.

"Yeah," he said, smoothing his hand over Sebastian's hair. "A little bit. But Dr. Stevens is awesome and I know his team will take really good care of us."

Nodding, Sebastian settled further into the pillow as his eyes drooped. Once he was asleep, Peter rolled over to catch Carrie watching them, face resting on her hands atop the pillow.

"You spying on us, Longwood?" he teased.

"It's just so sweet to see you two together." Tears glistened in her eyes.

"I want to hold you so badly," he whispered.

"I know. Once you recover, I'm going to hold you a lot. You deserve it after everything you're doing for our son."

They gazed at each other in the soft glow of the TV until her eyes slid closed and she began to lightly snore. Grinning at the soft sounds, he grabbed the remote, clicked off the TV, and joined them in slumber.

The next morning, Carrie was a whirlwind as she herded everyone to the hospital before the crack of dawn. Inside, she was a mess of frazzled nerves but knew she needed to project confidence and calm for her baby. Once Peter and Sebastian were in their gowns, resting comfortably in their pre-op hospital beds, she bolted to the lobby to grab some coffee. Noticing how badly her hand was shaking as she lifted the cup, she inhaled some deep breaths to calm the fear.

Once back in the pre-op area, she waited for Dr. Stevens to appear. He strolled around the corner with his effervescent smile and Carrie felt relief for the first time that morning.

"How are we doing, today?" Dr. Stevens asked, holding a tablet and clicking on it. "Are you both ready to help Sebastian get a shiny new kidney?"

"Ready!" they said in unison.

"Hey, Doc," Peter said, urging him closer with his hand. "Can you get me something hotter than this gown? I'm trying to win this one back and it's *reaaaaaally* unsexy."

"Peter!" Carrie said, slapping his leg as it rested under the covers.

Chuckling, Dr. Stevens nodded. "I'll see what I can do Peter. In the meantime, Dr. Crowley is going to give you both some medicine so you'll go to sleep. You'll be asleep the entire time we operate so I'll see you after the procedure, okay?" he asked Sebastian.

"Okay," he said, nodding.

"It will be several hours, Carrie, so once they're in surgery feel free to head to the café and work or grab something to eat. The nurse will call your cell when it's time to head back to the waiting room."

"Thank you so much for everything, Dr. Stevens," she said, tears welling in her eyes. "I can't imagine going through this with any other doctor."

"Of course," he said, rubbing her arm. "It's going to be fine. Our team does this every day, Carrie. I don't want you to worry."

"You know that's impossible when it's your child."

"That I do," he said, his eyes sparkling. "See you in a bit." Turning, he left the area and Carrie observed the anesthesiologist enter.

"We're going to start administering the anesthesia now, Ms. Longwood. Feel free to wish them well and then you can head to the waiting room."

Leaning over Sebastian's bed, she gave him a firm hug and placed a wet kiss on his lips. "I hope you have awesome dreams while you're asleep, sweetheart."

"I'm scared, Mommy."

He hadn't called her that in years and her heart clanked in her chest. "I know, baby, but Dr. Stevens is amazing and he's promised to take care of you. I need you to be strong for me, okay?" she asked, cupping his face.

He nodded and she wanted to melt into the floor at the tears that swam in his eyes.

"Hey, buddy, want to make a bet whose scar will be cooler?" Peter asked. "I think mine will because my stomach is bigger. What do you think?"

Sebastian pondered as he blinked the wetness away. "Mine might be because they have to take out my old kidney out and put yours back in."

Peter's gaze lifted to the ceiling as he contemplated. "Hmmm, maybe. I wonder whose will be redder and grosser?"

"Mine's going to be super-gross!" Sebastian exclaimed.

Standing there, as they both devolved into laughter, Carrie added the moment to one of the many she kept in her head as snapshots of the times she fell in love with Peter. There was the first time when Johnny Glendon had pulled out a huge chunk of her hair in fifth grade and Peter had punched his two front teeth straight out of his mouth.

The time in high school when Heather Combs had brushed her cheerleading-uniform-clad body against his in front of their lockers and told Peter she'd make out with him under the bleachers if he broke up with Carrie. Peter had pushed her away and strode toward Carrie, planting a huge kiss on her lips before telling Heather to fuck off.

The time when they lost their virginities to each other when they were about to turn eighteen. He'd gazed at her so reverently and told her he loved her so many times, the words had been emblazoned on her soul.

There was the time Peter came home after she broke up with Brandon and he held her close, assuring her she was better off without him. Brandon had started a false post-breakup rumor around town that Carrie gave him an STD. In retaliation, Peter had taken out an op-ed in the local paper where he interviewed several local business owners—the auto repair shop, the dry cleaner, and the pub—stating that Brandon had open tabs and never paid his bills. It was a bold move Carrie would've never even dreamed of but Peter had always been brash and he wanted to expose Brandon for the low-life liar he was. Brandon moved out of town three months later, never to be seen in Ardor Creek again.

More recently, there was the time when Peter had shown up at her house on his apology tour after his stint in rehab. He'd been so thin and contrite as he held her hand and begged for forgiveness. Although she'd vowed to hate him forever after their last terrible argument, she capitulated and bestowed her forgiveness, understanding she would always love him, despite his many transgressions.

And now, in the staid hospital ward, Carrie took one more snapshot, adding it to the memories. Peter, realizing their son was terrified and doing his best to distract him and make him laugh. Feeling her chin warble, she strode to his side and planted a smacking kiss on his lips.

"What was that for?" Peter asked, beaming up at her.

"Ask me after the surgery," she said, swiping away a tear. "I hope you have sweet dreams too."

"Carrie," he whispered, sliding his hand over her neck and tugging her close. Resting his lips against the shell of her ear, he whispered, "I love you. I always have. Just in case something happens, I needed to say it."

Clenching her lids, she strove to keep her knees from buckling at the poignant words. Of course, she longed to say them back, but Peter had tossed them in her face so many times, they failed to form on her lips.

"It's okay," he said, smiling at her as she rose. "One day, I'm going to earn those words back, honey."

Swallowing the lump in her throat, she squeezed his hand. "Sweet dreams, guys." Blowing them both one last kiss, she exited the room before she lost the will to do so.

Once downstairs in the café, she stared absently at the table, cherishing Peter's words as her hand rested over her anxious heart. Closing her eyes, she prayed for them to be okay as she began the arduous wait.

S everal hours later, Carrie was waiting in the post-op waiting room when Dr. Stevens appeared.

"Don't get up," he said, waving his hand as he walked over in his scrubs. "You'll need to wait another half hour until they're ready for you in holding. But everything went fine, Carrie. Both of them came through with flying colors and their vitals are excellent."

"Thank god," she said, breathing a sigh of relief. "I told myself not to be nervous but realized that was impossible the second I left pre-op."

"It's a normal reaction but you can relax now. Sebastian will be held in post-op before heading to ICU for a few days. Peter will be held in post-op before being taken to his assigned room. I do need to check on finding him a fancier hospital gown, though," he teased, rubbing his chin.

Chuckling, Carrie stood. "Can I hug you? Is that weird?"

"Of course," he said, embracing her. "Their recovery will be intense but manageable. Please call me if you need anything. We've already got Sebastian's post-op appointments scheduled for the next few months and I'll continue to check in before you take him home."

"Thank you. Will someone come and get me when I can see them?"

"Yes, Patricia, my Nurse Practitioner, will come get you when they're ready. In the meantime, I'm going to head to the café and grab a sandwich."

"Go, go," she said, waving her hand. "Sorry to keep you. You definitely deserve that sandwich."

Giving a nod, he thanked her and trailed away. Thirty minutes later, Patricia appeared and led Carrie to the ICU. Sebastian was just waking up and her heart leaped into her throat at the sight of her baby lying in the huge hospital bed with tubes and monitors attached.

"Hey, sweetie," she said, sitting on the side of the bed. "I'm here. You did such a good job."

He croaked out a sound, his eyes swollen and glazed, and Patricia cupped Carrie's shoulder. "We just removed the breathing tube so he's going to have trouble speaking."

Nodding, she cupped his cheek. "Don't try to say anything, okay? Mommy's here and I'm going to take care of you. I love you so much, baby."

He gave her a faint smile and her heart exploded in her chest. Closing her eyes, she thanked the lord above he was okay. After spending almost forty-five minutes with him, he began to drift off and she turned to Patricia. "Can I go see Peter now?"

"Yes, Carol will lead you to him," she said, gesturing with her head to a paper bonnet-clad nurse who gave her a warm smile.

"This way, Ms. Longwood."

Carol led her down a hallway, out of the ICU to another ward. Stopping at the third door on the right, she indicated for Carrie to step through.

"Peter?" she called, approaching the bed. "How are you feeling?"

"Hey, Care Bear," he said, his eyes appearing glassy. "I haven't been this high in years. *Whooooooo.* Where you been all my life?"

Snickering, she sat on the side of the bed and grasped his hand.

"Mr. Stratford had quite a strong reaction to the anesthesia," Carol said, checking the monitors beside the bed. "It affects some more than others. He's pretty loopy."

"Loopy? I'm not loopy. I'm freeeeee. Where was this stuff when I was going on benders? It's amazing."

Biting her lip, Carrie shot Carol a worried glance. "Will the anesthesia affect his sobriety? I know he discussed this with Dr. Crowley but want to make sure."

"The anesthesia Dr. Crowley used has no proven correlation to relapse in addicts so he should be just fine. It will be out of his system fairly soon. If you want to ask him anything, now's the time. That stuff is better than truth serum."

"He's been pretty honest with me this time around," she said, squeezing his hand, "so I actually have nothing to grill him about. Talk about a missed opportunity."

"Where's the sexy nurse uniform?" Peter asked, pouting. "I want the sexy nurse uniform."

Carol chuckled. "Stay as long as you like, Ms. Longwood. Your pass allows you to travel between the ICU and Mr. Stratford's room. If you have any questions, just come find me or Patricia."

"Will do. Thank you."

Once the nurse left, Carrie grinned at Peter. "I'm going to have to play the sexy nurse for you, aren't I? I don't think you're going to let it go."

"It's my only wish in the world. Sexy nurse and then I can die a happy man."

"Okay, no one's dying, but message received. Once we get home, I'll work on that."

Squeezing her hand, he stared at her with glassy eyes. "How's Sebastian?"

"He's good. He's pretty sluggish and just fell asleep so I came to check on you."

"I'm so glad he's okay. I love him, Carrie, and Charlie too."

"I know."

"I hate that they have that douchebag's last name. Let's name them Stratford. Longwood-Stratford. Like those stupid sweat-shirts we made in high school that had our last names on them."

"That's way down the road, Peter, and maybe not even on the map. We have a long way to go before we get to that point."

"I should've married you when we were eighteen. Should've told your dad to fuck off and just married you."

"That would've been a really bad idea. Age gives you perspective. Although I hate how much we hurt each other, maybe we needed to have our own experiences to become the versions of ourselves that can finally make this work."

"Maybe. Don't kick me out before I win you over, okay? I don't want to go back to that empty house. I like being with you and the boys."

"You're begging me to make you settle down in Ardor Creek. Wow, you really are loopy."

Inhaling, he closed his eyes. "Tired. Gonna pass out soon..." he mumbled.

"I'll come back to check on you," she said, standing and kissing his forehead. "Sweet dreams, Peter."

Thankful he was okay, she headed back to her son's room.

Chapter 14

♥

The next few days of recovery passed by in a flash. Ashlyn and Scott brought Charlie down to visit Sebastian and Peter on Sunday, and Peter was released on Monday morning. Carrie drove him home as he lay in the backseat grumbling that he wasn't twenty-five anymore and his body hated him.

"We'll get you settled into bed and all taken care of before I go back to sit with Sebastian this afternoon," she said into the rearview mirror. "You'll feel better once you rest and set a normal routine."

"Normal routine my ass," he muttered. "Give me the kidney back. I feel like crap."

Since he was an addict, he wasn't able to take any pain meds besides ibuprofen, and Carrie watched him swallow two pills before she settled him into the guest bed.

Grunting, he pulled the covers to his chin and ran his hand over his face. "It has to feel better tomorrow, right?"

"Yes," she said, stroking a tuft of hair off his forehead. "I'll be back in a few hours with dinner. Until then, try to get some rest. Ashlyn is on her way over to keep an eye on you. She's also agreed to clean and do the laundry, proving she's a saint."

She left him, grumpy and surly, and drove back to Scranton to sit with Sebastian. He'd moved out of ICU to a private room and Dr. Stevens informed her he was tolerating the kidney extremely well. If he continued to flourish, Dr. Stevens promised to release him on Tuesday afternoon. Relieved she wouldn't have to drive back and forth to Scranton much longer, she left Sebastian with the kind nurses and headed home to check on Peter.

They ate a light dinner together in the guest bedroom so Peter could remain in bed before he declared exhaustion and fell asleep. Carrie drove back to the hospital and spent the night while Scott stayed at Carrie's just in case.

By Tuesday evening, both of her boys were home and Carrie began the arduous task of ensuring their recovery. Sebastian needed to get used to the immunosuppressant medication, but he seemed to tolerate the pills without noticeable side effects. In fact, her son's recovery was rather uneventful, for which she was grateful.

Peter, on the other hand, was another story. As the days dragged on, he became churlish and annoyed at the lack of functionality of his body. Carrie assured him he needed to get up and move to feel better. They would take slow, measured walks around the yard as he leaned on her, muttering that he was an old man who should've never stopped taking drugs.

"I don't even want to hear you joke about that, Peter," Carrie scolded as they walked beside the small stream that ran behind her house one evening.

"Sorry," he said, sounding anything but. "I just hate this, Carrie. I don't want to be dependent on you."

Halting, she turned and cupped his face. "Peter," she said, her tone reverent. "You saved our baby. Don't you understand? I'll take care of you for a thousand years in exchange for that. I'm happy to do it."

Blue eyes roved over her. "I want to be strong for you. This is so lame."

"You had major surgery. Give yourself a break. You'll be back to normal in no time, especially if you check that bad attitude."

"You sound like my sponsors."

"Great. You seem to listen to your sponsors so listen to me. It's okay for you to show vulnerability, Peter."

"Last time I showed vulnerability, my dad beat my face in."

"That was a lifetime ago. We're different people now."

His lips formed a tender smile. "We are."

"If you're good, I might even consider the whole sexy nurse scenario. But I need you to be in prime condition so I can examine you." Trailing her fingers over his jaw, she ran her thumb over his lip. "Are you catching my drift here?"

"Yes," he said, nodding with excitement. "I'm healed. One hundred percent. Feel fantastic. See you tonight once the kids go to bed."

Throwing back her head, she laughed harder than she had in years. "Wow, that's a major turnaround."

Beaming, he palmed her cheek. "I promised myself I'd make you laugh that hard again one day. Damn, it feels good. I love seeing you laugh, Carrie."

"We used to laugh like that all the time. What the hell happened?"

"I became a dick and you married one. We fucked everything up royally."

"We sure did. Hopefully, our days of being idiots are over. Come on. I need to get the water boiling for the spaghetti."

Leading him inside, she prepped dinner and they dug in. Smacking his lips, Sebastian asked for seconds, proving he was well on his way to a full recovery. Although he spent most days resting, she was glad to see him sitting at the table and in good spirits. Soon, he would be back to her rambunctious child with limitless energy and a healthy body. Grateful, Carrie sent a silent prayer to the universe.

As the preacher's daughter, she'd attended church regularly when she was young. But her father had been strict and had detested Peter, creating a wedge in their father-daughter relationship. Eventually, she left the church behind but still believed in the moral teachings and hoped to bestow those values in her boys. Carrie firmly believed in her heart that one didn't need to attend services to be a kind, loving person. Decency was exhibited in a person's everyday interactions and intentions.

"I want tacos tomorrow," Charlie whined, dragging her from the musings. "We haven't had them in a long time."

"I had surgery so I get to pick the food," Sebastian exclaimed, puffing his chest out.

"Tacos sound awesome," Carrie said, shooting a warning glare at Sebastian. "I'll cook those for us tomorrow."

"Can we have chicken tacos too?" Sebastian asked. "I hate the beef ones."

"I'll cook chicken and beef since those are Charlie's favorite."

"I still win," Sebastian said, sticking out his tongue at his brother.

"It's not a contest, guys. Finish up so we can have ice cream."

Thankfully, the discussion turned to more benign topics and the boys eventually headed to bed. Exhausted, Carrie collapsed on the couch while Peter headed to the guest room to lie down and catch up on some work emails. Reveling in the silence, Carrie closed her eyes and relaxed back against the soft cushions of the couch.

Something tugged at her shoulder and she batted it away. "Leave me alone," she mumbled.

"You fell asleep on the couch, honey," Peter's baritone chimed in her ear. "I'd carry you to bed if it wouldn't rip my side open. You look pretty hot with that drool on your chin."

Glowering, she sat up and wiped her chin. "I hate you."

"There's the Carrie I remember. You always were a terror when you woke up."

"Why are you antagonizing me? I'm exhausted, Peter. Leave me alone."

Compassion laced his handsome features. "What can I do to help you, honey? I can't do much but I think I can manage a massage."

"I'm fine," she said, standing and running her hand through her hair. "You're the one who's recovering. I just need a good night's sleep."

"Remember that whole 'depending on someone' speech? I'm tempted to give it back to you. You can't shoulder the burden of two recovering surgery patients alone."

"I'm doing just fine, thank you." Rolling her neck, she yawned. "Let me get you into bed. Tomorrow will be better."

Once he was beneath the covers, she checked his scar and replaced the dressing as Patricia had taught her in the hospital. Giving him a peck on the forehead, she turned to leave.

"Carrie?"

"Yeah?" she asked, hand on the knob as she turned to face him.

Ocean blue eyes sparkled with emotion as he gazed at her. "You're amazing. See you in the morning."

Carrie couldn't contain her smile. He looked so adorable as he lay there in the bed, tired and recovering from the magnificent gift he'd bestowed upon their son. Vowing to reward him, she blew him a kiss and headed to her bedroom.

Once her teeth were brushed and she was comfortable in her PJs, she slid into bed and pulled up the shopping app on her phone. Scrolling through, she found a sexy nurse outfit and added it to her cart for next-day shipping. Yes, Peter had done so much for their son and she was ready to show him how thankful she was.

Anticipating his reaction, she clicked off the phone and fell into a deep slumber.

Chapter 15

♥

Two nights later, Peter lay in the bed, sleep a distant memory as his scar throbbed under the bandage. He thought he'd been prepared for the post-surgery recovery but he was in more pain than he'd anticipated. Pushing forty wasn't for the weary. Long gone were the days when he could party all night and barely have a hangover the next day. At the rate he was going, he might be holed up in Carrie's guest room for eternity...which wouldn't be half bad, in all honesty.

Something shuffled outside the bedroom door and Peter strained to listen in the dim room. The bedside lamp had a soft glow and he wondered if Carrie was still awake. There hadn't been any late-night visits to his bed since the surgery and he missed them with a voracious force that burned deep within.

Ever so slowly, the door creaked open and Peter's eyes widened as he focused on the vision before him. Carrie stepped inside, dressed in a white nurse's uniform that must've been sold from one of those sexy Halloween internet stores. A garter belt attached to thigh-high, white lace-topped hose covered long legs that stretched into black high heels. Thick, red hair fell below a small white nurse's hat and she softly clicked the door behind her.

"Mr. Stratford," she said, contemplating the clipboard she held as she bit the top of the pen. "I believe it's time for your check-up."

"Holy. Fucking. Shit." Although his body was a wreck, every ounce of blood surged to his dick as it swelled atop his abdomen. "Am I dreaming?"

"I don't know," she said, her tone sultry and low. "I thought it would be best to make sure a medical professional checks out *every inch* of your body. After all, Mr. Stratford, you've been through quite an ordeal with that big, bad surgery."

The sexy lilt in her voice made his body hum. "Well, Nurse Longwood, I'm ready for my physical." Resting his hands beneath his head on the pillow, he waited.

"That's good. I think you're going to be a very fun patient." Walking forward, she lifted her arm and slowly opened her fingers, dropping the pen to the carpet. "Oh, how silly of me. I dropped my pen. Let me pick that up." Turning to face the door, she bent over and Peter groaned from the mattress. She wasn't wearing any underwear beneath the cute little skirt and the folds of her pussy glistened as she bared herself.

"*Oh my god...*" he breathed, lowering his hand to cup his shaft.

Making a *tsk, tsk, tsk* sound, Carrie straightened and sauntered toward him. "Hands behind your head, Mr. Stratford. *I'll* be doing the touching for this exam. We wouldn't want you to open your scar."

"Yes, ma'am," he said, replacing his hand behind his head so quickly he wondered how it didn't fall off.

"Good boy," she said, stroking his cheek. Lifting her leg, she rested the heel of her sexy shoe beside him on the bed. "How are you feeling this evening?"

"My prognosis just got a lot better."

"Oh, I bet it did," she murmured, pretending to write on the clipboard. "Let me just jot that down."

Unable to resist, he reached toward her slick folds, open and bare to him as her foot balanced on the bed. Trailing his finger over her silken skin, he reached her opening and circled it.

"What did I tell you about using those hands?" she asked in that stern tone that drove him wild.

Gaze cemented to hers, he slid his finger inside her taut channel, loving the resulting flush on the pale skin below her neck. Lost in the magnificent dream which was somehow reality, he fucked her with his hand as she gazed at him through hooded lids. Licking those strawberry-pink lips, she began jutting back against him with small movements of her hips.

Dying to make her come, he inserted two fingers while resting the heel of his hand against her clit. Applying pressure to the swollen little bud, he surged inside her tight warmth, reveling in how she pushed against him. Hooking his fingers, he tapped against the spot he'd committed to memory, all those years ago when he used to play with her like this. Even when she'd guarded her virginity, she'd always let him play with her in other ways.

"*Oh, god...*" she cried.

"Reach for it, honey," he commanded, his voice gravelly. "Let me get you off."

Setting the clipboard on the bedside table, she leaned over him. Resting her palms flat on either side of his shoulders, she stared into his eyes. "I was going to make you come first," she whispered as she undulated against his hand.

"You're so fucking hot, Carrie. I love having you all over my fingers. Look at you, sweetheart..."

Throwing back her head, her mouth opened in a silent wail as she writhed atop his hand. She fucked him like a champ, stimulating herself by pushing into his firm pressure. Rubbing against his skin, she moaned his name and began to come, the muscles of her pussy squeezing his fingers. Peter almost felt his eyes cross at the sexy image as his body vibrated with unsated lust.

As the quivers died down, she lifted her head and gave him a sultry smile. "That was very naughty, Mr. Stratford. You're delaying me from performing my exam."

"By all means," he said, sliding from her and licking his fingers as she panted above. Placing his hand back behind his head, he smiled. "Exam away."

"Let's see," she said, stepping back to balance on one foot and tug off a heel before sliding off the other. "I think we need to examine your scar first." Dragging the sheet off his body, she stared at the pristine white bandage.

Concern entered her eyes as she touched him gently next to the scar. "Are you in a lot of pain?"

Wanting to ease her—and to get back to their sexy shenanigans—he shook his head. "It's fine, honey. I promise."

Green eyes searched his. "I'm so thankful you would put yourself through this to help Sebastian."

"I know," he said, reaching over and squeezing her wrist. "You're doing a *really* good job of showing me. Don't stop now."

Breathing a laugh, she slipped back into sexy nurse vibe. "Yes, sir, Mr. Stratford. I promise I'll take good care of you."

Trailing her fingers parallel to his scar, she stopped right before she reached his straining cock. "Oh, my, you're so swollen here." Her lips formed a wicked grin as she lightly ran her fingers over the soft skin of his shaft.

"Carrie..." he warned, hoping he didn't blow his load like a damn teenager.

"That's Nurse Longwood to you."

"Please, Nurse Longwood. It hurts."

Sliding those long legs over his, she straddled his thighs and grinned up at him. "I think I should kiss it and make it better."

"Holy shit," he breathed, clenching his teeth as she leaned over and ran the tip of her nose over the sensitive skin.

"Yes," she murmured, rubbing her lips over his cock as his eyes threatened to bug out of his head. "Let me kiss it and make it all better."

Grasping the base, she lifted him toward her mouth and extended her tongue, licking the straining head.

"Stop teasing me, honey," he pleaded.

Giving him a knowing grin, she shook her head. "This exam is performed at my pace, Mr. Stratford."

Exhaling a large breath, he lifted his hips, dying for her to take him inside that gorgeous, wet mouth.

She tortured him a while longer, licking the sensitive head before placing her lips around it. Gazing into him, she slid down his cock, slow and deliberate, her tongue creating exquisite pressure. Closing his eyes, Peter took a moment to settle into the bliss before focusing back on her.

She began to suck him in earnest, sliding up and down as her hand slid along the base. Pleasure coursed through every cell in his body as he watched her take his cock deep into her mouth. Unable to control his arms, they reached for her, tugging the silly cap from her head. Thrusting his fingers into her hair, he commanded, "Suck me hard, honey."

She complied, gripping his shaft as she worked herself over his straining cock. Saliva dripped from those swollen lips, lubricating the skin beneath her hand, and Peter saw stars. Jutting into her with hips he could no longer control, he struggled to breathe.

"I'm going to come in that pretty mouth," he gritted, tugging her hair. "Pull back now if you don't want that."

She sank further into him, sucking his cock to the back of her throat, spurring an intense groan from deep in his chest. Surging into her throat, he felt his balls tighten and knew he was close. She moaned and purred against his quivering skin, the sounds sending erotic bursts of pleasure through his body as they reverberated off the walls in the small room.

Screaming her name, he began to come, spurting hot, sticky jets of release into her wet mouth. Mewling around his shaft, she lapped up every single drop, still jerking the base as he emptied himself. Throwing his head back on the pillow, he reveled in the release, unable to control his sated shouts of pleasure.

"Shhh..." she said, chuckling against the sensitive skin as she drew back. "You'll wake the kids."

"Kids? What kids? Are we still on Earth? I'm pretty sure I transported to another universe."

Laughing, she kissed a trail up the unblemished side of his abdomen, taking a love bite from his turgid nipple before settling into his good side. Leaning on her hand as her elbow dug into the bed, she smiled as she caressed his jaw.

"It felt good?"

"Jesus, Carrie, yes."

She rubbed her silken covered leg over his. "Was it everything you imagined? You were pretty set on the sexy nurse fantasy. Figured you earned it since you gave up a major organ."

Inhaling through his nostrils, unable to regulate his breathing, he stroked the hair at her temple, overcome with how gorgeous she was. Red hair sat strewn atop her head from his earlier ministrations and her lips were swollen and wet.

"I couldn't have imagined it any better," he whispered, running his thumb over her lip. "I've missed you, Carrie."

"I'm right here."

"I've missed you sneaking into my room when it's dark," he said, winking.

"So have I." Snuggling into him, she rested her head into the juncture between his neck and shoulder. Tracing her finger beside his scar, she asked, "How are you feeling, really? I want to make sure you're okay."

"I'm good," he said, kissing her hair as he stroked her shoulder. "It's not a bed of roses but being here with you and the boys helps."

As if on cue, a voice chimed outside the door.

"Mom? Can I have some Kool-Aid? Sebastian drank it all and there's only a little bit left."

Carrie sucked in a breath and lifted on straight arms as she gaped at the closed door.

"Charlie? How did you know I was in here?"

"I heard Uncle Peter's voice. It was loud. Can I come in?" The doorknob began to turn.

"Don't come in!" Carrie yelled, scrambling off the bed. "You can go to the kitchen and pour the rest of the Kool-Aid. Mom needs to...uh..." she looked at her disheveled clothing, "...change into new pajamas upstairs and then I'll make more, okay?"

"Okay."

Her eyes darted around the room as she listened for sounds of him walking away.

"Busted," Peter said, waggling his brows.

"*This* is why I haven't been sneaking into your room. They hear everything!" she hissed.

Reaching over, he grabbed her wrist and pulled her to sit on the bed.

"Maybe we should talk about making this more serious. If we take the next step I can move into your room. I'm pretty sure it has a lock and this room definitely doesn't."

Sighing, she ran a hand through her hair. "I'm not having this discussion at midnight when my kid's in the kitchen."

Hurt washed over him as he frowned, feeling dismissed.

"But we'll have it one day soon, okay?" Leaning down, she kissed him. "Don't be surly."

"I want you to stay," he pouted.

Straightening, she rolled her eyes. "Whining doesn't work on a mom of two, Peter. I'm immune. You should have figured that out by now." Striding to the door, she peeked outside, making sure the coast was clear and turned back to blow him a kiss.

Catching it, he blew her one back before she breezed out the door, closing it behind. Settling back into the bed, Peter exhaled a satisfied sigh, hoping he'd dream of her in that sexy as hell costume as soon as he fell asleep.

Chapter 16

♥

By mid-June, Peter and Sebastian were well on their way to recovery. The pain had lessened over time and Peter was thankful his weary body was finally healing. Thoroughly convinced that Carrie's sweet, sexy loving was helping, he urged her to come to his room as often as possible. Although she didn't appear every night, she did sneak in with measured regularity which gave him hope. Now that he'd had a taste of living with her and the boys, he was hooked. Perhaps it was the addict inside, but being part of their family was the greatest high he'd ever experienced and he desperately wanted to make it permanent.

In July, he returned to work and the increased activity also lifted his spirits. One day, as he was sitting at Scott's desk reviewing the finances on his computer, his friend strolled into the office.

"Nice to see you up and about, buddy," Scott said, folding into one of the chairs in front of his desk. "How are you feeling?"

"Pretty damn awesome," Peter said, leaning back and threading his hands behind his head. "It was rough for a while there but I think I'm almost back to a hundred percent."

"Glad to hear it. Carrie says Sebastian's doing great too. They're in Scranton for a follow-up today."

"Yep, he seems fine. The medication he's on has a few mild side effects but he just plows on. Must be his superior genes."

Chuckling, Scott nodded. "How are you handling that bombshell by the way? Does it feel strange to realize you have a son?"

Compressing his lips, Peter contemplated. "I was floored at first, believe me, but it wasn't as shocking as you'd think. I've engaged in a ton of deep reflection since rehab and realized I should've married Carrie years ago. I thought the door was closed because I fucked up so badly but this opened it again so I'm really thankful."

"I thought you blew it too."

"Thanks," Peter muttered.

Breathing a laugh, he shrugged. "I mean, you were a total dick, man, but that secret was a whopper. You've been really great about forgiving her."

"I left her with no choice," he said, running his hand over his face. "Her actions make complete sense. I don't want to waste time being angry but I am really sad I missed being his dad for all these years."

"How is it so far? Do you enjoy being a dad?"

"Love it," he said, beaming. "I can see parts of myself in him and it's so damn cool. He rubs the back of his neck when he's thinking, just like I do, and he has a tiny dimple when he smiles right here." Peter pointed to his own dimple. "It's so strange and daunting and amazing, all at the same time."

"That's great, Peter. I'm so happy for you."

"I love Charlie too. Even though he's not my biological child, I see so many of Carrie's traits in him. He's kind and loving but also assertive and really smart. They're amazing kids and she's done such a good job raising them."

"So, what's the next step? Are you going to propose?"

Sighing, he lifted a shoulder. "I don't know. I want to but we have a long way to go before we get there. I'm pretty sure she's going to ask me to move home now that I'm recovered, which really sucks."

"Can't you talk her into trying to live together?"

"I'm going to talk to her tonight once the kids go to sleep. She seems hesitant and doesn't want to confuse the boys. I've told her a hundred times that I still love her but she hasn't said it back yet."

Scott lifted a brow. "It's obvious she loves you, Peter. That's not even in question."

"Yes, but that doesn't mean she's ready to trust me or open herself up again. I get it. I treated her like shit for so long." Narrowing his eyes, he absently chewed his lip. "I'm also determined not to make worthless promises to her this time around. A part of me is worried I'll fall off the wagon and let them all down. It's one of the reasons I stayed away after her divorce. But as terrified as I am of failing them, circumstances changed when I learned Sebastian was mine. I'm ready to jump in and do my best to make it work."

"You're finally ready to commit and she's not having it."

"Yep," Peter said, laughing. "We always did have a hard time getting on the same page."

"Well, I wish you luck. Carrie's tough as nails but I think you can wear her down if you focus."

"Hope so." Straightening, he leaned his forearms on the desk. "On that note, part of my whole commitment strategy is showing her I'm willing to put down roots here. She's mentioned to me a few times that she wonders if I'll want to move back to the city now that Mom's passed away. In the interest of making things more permanent, I think I'm ready for you to build that office for me."

"Yeah?" Scott asked, grinning. "I can renovate the back room pretty quickly. I'd love for you to have a permanent office here, Peter."

"It will be good because I can meet my accounting clients there too. I usually go to their homes or meet them at the diner, but an office is certainly more professional."

"And you'll get to work with Carrie every day." Scott gave him a knowing look.

"Doesn't hurt, for sure. Maybe it will increase my opportunities to woo her."

"I'm all for it," Scott said, standing. "I'll reach out to Chad about the permits and get to work on it next week."

"Thanks, man," Peter said, walking around the desk. "What's Ashlyn cooking in the truck this week? I'm starving."

"Pulled pork tacos. They're amazing. Come on, let's grab some."

Exiting the office, Peter patted him on the back, grateful for his enduring friendship.

That evening, as Carrie was putting the boys to bed, Peter cleaned up the kitchen and poured her a glass of wine. When she breezed into the room, he handed it to her and she arched a brow.

"A pristine kitchen *and* a glass of wine?" she asked, taking a sip. "You must really want sex tonight."

Chuckling, he took her hand and led her to the living room couch. Once they were seated, Peter pulled her outstretched leg on his lap as her other leg bent beneath her. Gently massaging her foot, his body immediately hardened at her sexy moan.

"Okay, you definitely want something *in addition* to sex. Keep doing that and you'll most likely get it."

Feeling his lips curve, he took stock of the gorgeous picture she presented, relaxed and cozy on the couch with hair trailing from the soft bun atop her head. Peter had always thought her so stunning and she'd only grown into her beauty with age.

"Okay, you're staring. I feel like you're trying to count the freckles on my face like you used to in high school."

"Your freckles are so damn adorable. I've always thought so."

"You seem to like the ones on my body even more than the ones on my face," she said in a sultry tone.

"I think I've kissed every single freckle on every inch of your body at this point and I love them all equally."

"Okay, Mr. Super Sappy, give it to me. What are you buttering me up for?"

Working his thumb around her arch, he felt his heartbeat accelerate. Trying to calm the nerves, he stared into her eyes. "I want to move in for real, honey."

Her spine straightened and the easy smile disappeared. Squeezing her foot, he shook his head. "Please don't tense up. I think I can make a really good case if you'll hear me out."

Rubbing her forehead with her fingers, she appeared annoyed. "I'm not ready, Peter. There's so much to consider, I wonder if you've even begun to contemplate it."

"Like what? Making sure the boys are on board? I'm sure they would be."

"Yes, but it would be a huge change for them—"

"We've done fine since the surgery—"

"Don't interrupt me," she said, dragging her foot away and straightening. "I won't be talked over if we're going to have this conversation."

"Fine," he said, clenching his jaw. "Go on."

Inhaling, she set the glass on the table before clenching her hands in her lap, fingers fidgeting. "One man has already left them and he's never coming back. That's a choice I made and I struggle with. Part of me thinks it's awful I don't encourage them to see Jeff, but he hasn't made any attempts to see them either. That proves what a shithead he is. I remind myself of this when I'm beating myself up over denying them from having a father."

"Do you not think I would be a good dad, Carrie? I know I fucked up but if you believe that, it really hurts. I would do anything for them."

"I know you would put them first in the beginning," she said, holding up a finger when anger entered his expression. "And I know you would have every intention of staying. But you've always chased shiny new things and I worry what will happen once the luster has worn off. Being a parent is excruciatingly difficult and soul-crushing half the time. It's not something you can do in half-measures."

"I'm trying really hard not to tell you to go to hell right now, Carrie. I can't believe you're accusing me of loving them in half-measures."

"Being Uncle Peter is fun but it doesn't bear the responsibility of being 'Dad'. That's a whole other level you've never experienced. You can't just rush in headfirst. You need to really contemplate if you want to give up your life because you'll have a very different life with two kids."

"You make it look so easy," he said, shrugging. "Maybe I have no idea because you're so damn good."

"I developed a stiff upper lip because I had to but, believe me, there are nights I cry myself to sleep because I'm at the end of my rope. Being a parent makes you doubt everything about yourself and there are times where you think really awful thoughts and feel terrible for them afterward."

"How awful?"

She gnawed her lip before continuing. "A few months ago, I remember thinking I wanted to drive Sebastian to the homeless shelter and leave him there so he could see how lucky he was to live in such privilege. He'd spent all day whining about not getting a new video game he wanted and I swear, Peter, for ten seconds, I imagined leaving him there and running away forever."

"Yikes," he said, grimacing.

"Yeah. Of course, I regained my sanity and spent the next three hours inwardly berating myself for being such a terrible mom."

"You're not terrible," he said, scooting over and sliding his arm around her shoulders. "You're just human, Care Bear."

"Yeah," she said, placing her head on his shoulder. "I guess so. Regardless, I can't let you just move in and upend their lives. If I consider this, it needs to be done thoughtfully."

"Okay," he said, nuzzling her hair, hating he couldn't just forge full steam ahead. "I understand, although I hate it. I'm done living in my mom's house. I want to sell it and settle down with you."

"That's also pretty tough to believe. I'm going to have to process whether I truly think you're ready to stay and commit to us. I know that probably seems shitty after you donated a major organ to our son but a lifelong commitment is intense, Peter. You've never been able to make one to me before."

Lifting her chin with his fingers, he stared into her eyes. "I know. I was always so afraid of committing to you, which was always incongruent with my feelings. One never had anything to do with the other."

"Love was so easy for us," she said softly, caressing his jaw. "It's all the other stuff that was really hard."

Nodding, he ran his thumb over her cheek. "I hate that you don't trust me. It fucking kills me."

"It kills me too. Hopefully, I'll figure out a way to learn to trust you again. You're going to have to be patient with me."

"How patient? I'm only asking because we're pushing forty here."

Carrie snickered. "Well, hopefully, it doesn't take me four more decades."

Glancing at the ceiling, he murmured, "I think I'd look pretty hot in adult diapers."

"Gross." Swatting his chest, she relaxed against him.

"Okay, hon, I'll move home and work like hell to earn you. But I want to make something clear: I'm determined to be in your life. I want to marry you and adopt the boys and build our life together."

"That's so sweet. It warms my heart that you love my two heathens."

"They're great kids. Honestly, they make me want more."

Craning her neck, she gave him an incredulous look. "More kids?"

"Yeah," he said, chuckling at her expression. "I mean, why not? We could try to have a girl this time with your red hair and cute freckles. She'd be adorable."

Pointing at her stomach, she said, "You know this uterus is only months away from forty, right?"

Throwing back his head, he laughed. "Yes. I love that you're the older woman."

"By three months," she muttered.

"If you're open to trying, I'd have another one with you, Carrie. It would give me the chance to experience everything I missed with Sebastian."

Her eyes darted between his. "I denied you those years. I'm so sorry, Peter. I deeply regret keeping him from you."

"I know," he said, swiping a wisp of hair off her forehead. "I blame myself as much as you. I made it impossible for you to feel safe enough to tell me. But I want to make up for it moving forward."

Sucking in a breath, she nodded. "All right. Let's do this thoughtfully and carefully. Even though you'll be living at home, we'll make a schedule so you can see the boys. I'm going to ask you to help me drive them to practices and events, help with homework, and that sort of stuff. It will definitely be more intense than playing Avengers and munching pizza. Are you ready for that?"

"Ready," he said, giving a salute. "And I'm also ready to sweep you off your feet."

"Sure. Circle back to me on that once you've done 'dad duty' for a week. It's exhausting. You'll be lucky if your body doesn't collapse."

"If I'm ever too tired to make love to you, please lock me up and destroy the key."

Laughing, she bit her lip. "I'm glad you're still into me. I have a few more wrinkles than when we were seventeen."

"I was just thinking how stunning you were when we sat down." He traced a finger along her jaw as he gazed at her. "You get prettier every day, honey."

Her nose scrunched. "That's kind of cheesy."

"It's true, woman. Leave me alone."

"You're pretty hot too. I think you're aging backward. It's disconcerting. You're Benjamin Buttoning me."

"I'll be into you even when you look like a grandma and I look like Zac Efron."

Rolling her eyes, she stood and extended her hand. "Okay, grandpa, bang me one last time before I kick you out so we can remember how it was before we needed walkers."

Grasping her hand, he stood and threaded their fingers. "I'm ready for this, Carrie. I can't wait to show you."

"Me either." Tugging his hand, she led him to the guest room. Cherishing the last night in her house—for now, at least—he held her close and vowed to win her heart all over again.

Chapter 17

♥

P eter moved back into his home and felt the loss of the family he'd come to love immediately. The silence was deafening as he attempted to sleep every night and he craved Carrie's soft body in the cold bed. Determined to prove his intention to fully commit, he leaped into action.

Now that Sebastian was fully recovered, the boys were involved in a plethora of activities. Sebastian enrolled in a summer baseball league, along with a soccer league in which Charlie played as well. Charlie also began piano lessons twice a week at Mrs. Connaughton's house. She was the retired music teacher from their local middle school and had always treated Peter fondly.

"How lovely to see you dropping off Charlie," Mrs. Connaughton said one Wednesday afternoon before the lesson. "Several little birdies around town told me you're trying to win Carrie over."

"In a town this small, I'm sure they know our favorite position at this point, Mrs. Connaughton," Peter said, grinning.

"Oh, you still have that dirty mouth, boy," she said, swatting him on the arm. "I'll let it slide if you promise to take care of that girl. You two were always meant for each other in my opinion. I still remember when I found you both in the instrument closet in eighth grade. Very naughty, young man." She gave a *tsk, tsk, tsk.*

"We were just cleaning the instruments' pipes, Mrs. C," he said, winking.

"That's enough." She gave him a playful glare before bending down to address Charlie. "You ready to show me what you learned?"

"I learned all the chords you gave me as homework," Charlie said, nodding.

"Excellent," she said, leading him to the piano. "Can't wait to hear. Peter, you can come back in an hour."

"Bye, Uncle Peter!" Charlie called. Looking up at Mrs. Connaughton, he said, "Uncle Peter is Sebastian's real dad but he's not mine. But Mom says he loves me just as much as Sebastian."

"I'm sure that's true," she said, cupping his cheek.

"Bye, Charlie," Peter said, his heart swelling at their conversation. "I'll see you in an hour."

While Charlie completed the lesson, Peter drove to the grocery store and undertook the task of purchasing everything on Carrie's massive list. She'd warned him that a family with two growing boys consumed a ton of food but the mission was daunting. Every food had a specific organic label or flavor and it took him the entire hour to ensure he purchased the correct items. Once finished, he picked up Charlie and headed to Carrie's house with grocery bags in tow.

As Carrie unpacked the groceries, Peter watched her, hoping he hadn't blown it. She wasn't kidding about this whole parenting thing being hard. He'd been helping her for less than two weeks and all he wanted was to sink into the couch and watch basketball while he decompressed. Turning to him, she lifted the can of black beans.

"These were supposed to be low sodium but that's okay. It's important I keep extra salt out of Sebastian's diet. Just a reminder for next time."

"When did food become so specific?" he asked, rubbing the back of his neck. "We used to eat hot dogs and milkshakes every day in high school."

"Times have definitely changed but it's important they eat as healthy as possible while still eating kid stuff from time to time."

"Am I going to get dinged for getting the wrong type of beans? Because I swear, I triple checked the list."

Grinning, she trailed over and cupped his face. "You did a great job. It's really cute to see how hard you're trying. I'm tempted to ask you to do things I don't even need just to see if you will."

"You evil woman," he said, sliding his hands to grip the globes of her ass through her tight jeans. "You're enjoying the hell out of this."

Closing her eyes, she inhaled as joy laced her features. "It's fucking fantastic."

Chuckling, he lowered his forehead to hers. "How long do I have to suffer? I miss you, Carrie."

"You're not even two weeks in, buddy." Disentangling, she resumed unpacking the groceries. "Let's give it some time."

Peter's lips formed a pout.

"But you're so damn adorable when you pout like that. You look so much like Sebastian."

"Adorable enough to sleep over?"

Laughing, she shrugged. "If you help me get them to bed at a reasonable hour, we can have some sexy times in the guest room before you go home. How's that?"

"Boys! Time for bed!"

"Shhh..." she said, slapping his shoulder. "It's six-fifteen, Peter. Good grief. I need to get the chili on. We'll eat at seven and you can play the new video game with them before they go down at eight-thirty."

"Bedtime, eight-thirty. Got it. Longest two hours of my life but I've got it."

"Get out of here," she said, shooing him away. "They're playing wiffleball outside. Go play with them."

Giving her a salute, he headed to play with the boys until she called them in for dinner. Afterward, Peter was given a full tutorial on the new video game before the boys went to bed. Carrie informed him she needed to fold the clothes in the dryer before they could hang so he sat on the couch and turned on the game. Minutes later, he was asleep.

He awoke to the magnificent sight of Carrie's lithe body sliding over his as she snuggled into his side. Pulling her close, he rested his cheek on her hair as she relaxed against him.

"Fell asleep," he mumbled.

"Mmm-hmm..." she warbled against his chest.

"We're supposed to be banging now, right?"

"Mmm-hmm..."

"In a minute."

Nodding, she snuggled deeper into his body as sleep settled back in. Several hours later, when he awoke, he carried her upstairs and placed her in bed, positioning the covers around her.

"Did we have sex? I can't remember."

"Very funny," he said, kissing her forehead. "You weren't kidding about the whole 'parent exhaustion' thing."

"Tried to tell you," she said, eyes heavy with slumber.

"Night, honey. I'll be back tomorrow to take the kids to soccer practice so you can have dinner with Ashlyn."

"Thanks. I'm excited to plan her baby shower."

Rising, he approached the door and she softly called his name. "Yes?"

"I appreciate how hard you're trying. Give me a few more weeks. Just need to make sure you understand what you're signing up for."

"If there's anything I've learned from my sobriety, we all have to take important steps at our own pace. But we're a team, hon. I know you'll believe that one day soon."

"I'm already starting to believe it," she said, burrowing into the covers. "Night, Peter."

"Night, honey."

Locking the house behind him, Peter headed home to get some sleep before the exhausting cycle began anew tomorrow.

The next evening, Carrie met Ashlyn for dinner at the pub. They gave each other a warm embrace before settling into the tall chairs at the high-top table.

"You're absolutely glowing, Ashlyn. How are you feeling?"

"Pretty awesome," she said, rubbing her distended abdomen. "Since I'm almost seven months, I figured the belly might take over, but it hasn't been too bad."

"You look great. Must be all the running you do with Scott and the runner's club."

"I'm still waiting for you to join," she said, arching her brows. "We'd love to have you."

"I've never been a runner unless you count chasing two rambunctious boys around. That zaps all my energy."

"I certainly understand that. Although it seems like you've had some help lately. Peter's really stepping up to the plate."

"I know," she sighed, smiling like a lovesick teenager, resting her chin on her hand as her elbow sat on the table. "I dreamed for so many years he'd come home and beg me to marry him. Eventually, I gave up and told myself I was living in fantasyland. Now, when I have extra cellulite and two heathens, he's ready to commit. Doesn't make a damn bit of sense."

Chuckling, Ashlyn shrugged. "I guess stuff needs to evolve over time. I certainly learned that with Scott. All the pain we experienced in our past somehow led us here." She pointed at her stomach. "I mean, holy shit. I'm pregnant."

"You certainly are, sweetie," she said, squeezing her wrist. "Let's order some food and we'll get down to planning."

"Thank you for doing this for me, Carrie. I'm so grateful you all have accepted me in Ardor Creek."

"Are you kidding? You saved us from Scott's excessive grumpiness. He's practically the life of the party these days. We should be thanking *you*."

"I'm so glad he's happy," she said wistfully. "But I kinda miss the surliness. It was pretty sexy."

"Oh, I'm sure he can turn it on when you need it, honey."

"Damn straight," she murmured, huffing on her nails and rubbing them on her shoulder.

They ordered dinner from Terry, the server who'd worked at the pub for years, and settled into planning. Ashlyn had a list of friends from the city she wanted to come as well as her mother and cousins.

"I also want to invite Tina's mother," she said, swallowing a bite of her salad. "I don't know how she'll receive it and it might be totally weird, but I just feel a calling to do it."

"Roslyn loved Scott and she still does. I know he thinks she blames him for the accident but I never believed that was true.

It was just hard for her to deal with losing her daughter and granddaughter."

"I can't even imagine," Ashlyn said, sitting back in her chair and rubbing her belly. "I already love this little peanut more than anything in the entire universe. A loss like that is utterly devastating. But there's always joy in celebrating new life and I hope she'll come. I'd really like to meet her and give her a huge hug."

"We'll definitely invite her, then. I've already talked to Frank and he's giving us the back room at Antonio's the day of the shower. Bill from Wine and Spirits is going to throw in some champagne so we can make mimosas. Terry and I will decorate." Checking everything off on the notebook she'd brought, she gave a nod. "I think we're pretty much set. Since the shower is in mid-September, I'll send the invites out next week."

"You're amazing, Carrie. Thank you so much."

"Of course. Having your first baby is such a special time. I remember when I was pregnant with Sebastian. Jeff hadn't morphed into full asshole yet and I have some good memories."

Ashlyn's eyes narrowed. "Your face just got all weird," she said, circling her hand over her face. "What are you thinking?"

Biting her lip, Carrie shook her head. "It's nothing. Just...well, Peter mentioned to me that he'd like to have another child. I was completely floored. You have to understand, this man never wanted anything remotely close to babies and commitment. I'm starting to think he's some sort of secret government test subject and they've replaced his brain with someone else's."

"Okay, first of all, I love the creativity," Ashlyn said, holding up a finger. "But maybe he just changed, Carrie. Sometimes people do. Especially with everything he went through to get sober. That can really transform someone."

"I know," she said, sighing. "I'm being pretty tough on him. It's probably a bit excessive but he made so many promises and told me so many lies, Ashlyn. I swore I'd never let him hurt me like that again."

"I don't blame you for protecting your heart. I say, make him sweat. He says he wants to win you back so let him do it. You deserve to be swept off your feet, Carrie."

"I mean, he did donate a major organ to our son."

"Yep. And now he has to prove he's ready to be a husband and father. Add it all together and I think you've got your happy ever after."

Scoffing, she said, "I gave up on that notion years ago."

"Well, I think you should reconsider," she said, eyes sparkling.

"Maybe I will." Lifting their glasses, they toasted to happy ever after and good health. After dinner, Carrie headed home, blood thrumming in anticipation of seeing Peter. Stepping inside the dim house, she found him watching basketball on the couch.

"Hey," he said, glancing up as she stepped between him and the TV. "Did you have fun with Ashlyn?"

Grabbing the hem of her shirt, she tugged it over her head before removing her bra.

Peter's eyes grew wide as he sucked in a breath. "I just put the boys to bed," he whispered.

Straddling him, she sank her fingers into his hair. "Then we'll have to be quiet. I owe you a solid bang in the guest room." Leaning forward, she rested her straining nipple against his lips.

Groaning, he sucked the sensitive bud inside his mouth before he carried her to bed and damn near took her to heaven. Later, as they lay entwined, sweaty and replete, Carrie recalled her conversation with Ashlyn. Was it possible to finally embrace happiness with Peter after all their heartache and pain? Snuggling into him as he tenderly caressed her hair, she let the notion sink in.

Holding him close, she decided to speak to the boys over the next few days and judge their reactions. If all went well, she would ask him to move in. Fear flared deep in her heart at the thought. After all, it would leave her wide open to another desertion if he eventually changed his mind. But there, in the soft bed surrounded by his strong arms, she closed her eyes and realized she just didn't give a damn. Her love for Peter somehow outweighed the fear, especially with everything he'd done for the boys over the past months.

Steeling her heart, Carrie nestled into her lover's body and finally allowed herself to imagine her very own happy ever after.

Chapter 18

On Saturday, Carrie called the boys into the living room before dinner. They'd had a busy day, filled with sports and a friend's birthday party, but were still somehow full of energy. Asking them to sit on the couch, she slid into the corner and smiled.

"I have something really important I want to discuss with you. Sebastian, please put that on the table while we talk."

Rolling his eyes, he set the handheld video game on the table. "I just started a new level."

"You can play it when we're done talking." Straightening, she sifted her fingers through Charlie's hair since he was closest. "I want to ask you both about Uncle Peter. It seems like you enjoy having him around. Is that right?"

They both nodded excitedly. "I'm happy he's my real dad and he's so fun when he comes to my practices."

"Charlie?"

"I like him, Mom. I wish he was my real dad too."

"Well, that's what I want to discuss with you guys. Real dads aren't just made from having the same genes. Peter loves you both a lot and wants to move in here with us. Eventually, if things go well, we'll get married and he'll adopt you and become your dad. How would you feel about that?"

"He can't be Charlie's dad because he doesn't have his genes," Sebastian said.

"That's not true. Being a dad is about how much you love someone and Peter loves both of you. Understood?"

"Yes," they said in unison.

"Good. I'm ready to ask Peter to move in and live with us but only if you both want him to live here. It's only been the three of us for a while now and I don't want to do anything that makes you feel uncomfortable."

"I want him to move in!" Charlie said, excitement glowing in his brown eyes. "He's really fun and plays with us all the time."

"We already know you *looooove* him, Mom," Sebastian said. "Just marry him already."

Laughing at her son's wise observation, she bit her lip. "Is it that obvious?"

"Yes," Sebastian said, beaming. "He's way better than our real dad. He should definitely move in."

"Okay, then, I think we've got a consensus."

"When are you going to get married?" Charlie asked.

"One day when we decide we're *all* ready. This will be a family decision, okay?"

They both gave an excited nod.

"Awesome. No matter what, I'll always love you both more than anyone or anything in the world. You know that, right?"

"Yes, Mom," they droned.

Chuckling, she extended her arms, pulling them into a huge bear hug as they crawled over her lap. Holding them close, she placed sweet kisses on their foreheads, excited for the future that lay ahead.

S unday evening, Carrie sat across from Peter at the pub as they finished dinner. Kara was babysitting and Carrie was thoroughly enjoying an evening out with her handsome date.

"Want another one, sweetie?" Terry asked as she approached, noticing her almost empty wine glass.

Pondering, Carrie chewed her lip since she'd already had two glasses.

"I'll drive home," Peter said, even though they'd driven her car. "Come on, you deserve it. I finally understand what it's like to be a parent. How are you all not drunk twenty-four-seven?"

"It's a struggle, believe me," Terry muttered, arching a brow. "Pinot grigio?"

"Sure," Carrie said, shrugging. "One more then cut me off."

When she sauntered away, Carrie smiled at Peter.

"What's that for? You're smiling a lot tonight, hon. What's cooking in that busy brain?"

"I spoke to the boys," she said, pushing the plate away and resting her chin on her hand as she gazed at him. "They're on board with you moving in."

His eyes grew wide as joy seeped into his expression. "Yeah? And how does their mom feel about it?"

Inhaling deeply, she lifted a shoulder. "Honestly, I'm terrified. But I'm also really excited. This is it, Peter. If you leave me again, I'll most likely hunt you down and devise some sort of really excruciating torture plan."

"Yikes," he said, grimacing.

"You wouldn't just be leaving me this time. You'd be leaving our boys. I hope you understand I'm not making this decision lightly. But I do think you've changed and I'm betting on the fact you care about us enough to stay."

"I *love* you guys, Carrie," he said, reaching over and lacing his fingers through hers atop the table. "I know I've done a terrible job at proving that until recently but it will be different this time."

Her eyes darted between his. "I think I'm finally starting to believe that after all these years."

Smiling, he rubbed his thumb over the soft skin of her hand. "Do you think you might tell me you love me back one of these days?"

Staring into his eyes, she wondered why the words still failed to form on her lips. They were inexorably true but she felt a deep resistance toward voicing them for some reason. Wrestling with the struggle deep within, she squeezed his hand.

"One day soon," she said softly.

Shaking his head, he gave her the adorable, sad smile Sebastian bestowed when he realized she was having a frazzled mommy moment and needed a hug. "Okay, hon. Man, you're tough. Can't wait," he said, winking.

Terry dropped off the wine and removed their plates. Peter ordered a tiramisu for them to share and she settled into the feeling of being pleasantly drunk.

"I'm going to put my house on the market next week," he said, finishing the last bite of tiramisu. "You okay with that?"

"Yep," she said, setting down the fork and relaxing back into the chair. "You're finally going to make it to the master bedroom. Nice job."

"I can't wait to lock that door and christen it, honey."

"Oh, I bet you can't. The boys are so excited, Peter. They love you so much. I told them you want to be their dad in every way. I hope you're ready for this."

"I'm so ready. I swear, Carrie."

"Good. You can start moving in tomorrow if you have time between clients. We'll have to figure out how to organize everything since I'm already convinced the house is too small. I'm not sure how a four-bedroom home can be too small but somehow it is."

"You were smart to snatch up the house when the development was new. Now it's worth three times what you paid for it."

"Jeff was against buying it but I forged ahead. We were barely able to secure the mortgage with our combined incomes. He sold his half to me when we divorced in exchange for not paying child support."

"What a dick."

"Honestly, it was the best thing. I got to keep our house and purge his toxicity from our lives. I'm thrilled with how it worked out."

"Well, Mom paid off her house years ago so I'll get a nice chunk from the sale. I can use it to pay down the principal on your mortgage and also put some in the boys' college funds."

The words all but melted her heart. "That's very sweet."

"They're our boys, Carrie. I told you, I'm going to adopt them but I want to marry you first."

Hiccupping since she was tipsy, she hid a giggle. "Sorry. I still reel every time you say stuff like that."

He gave a playful eyeroll. "One day it won't seem so impossible, I guess. I want you all to have my last name, Carrie. I know that's some ancient caveman shit and probably not progressive at all, but it's what I want. Are you open to that?"

"Since I used to doodle Carrie Elizabeth Stratford on every notebook I owned in high school, I guess I could get on board with it."

Chuckling, he gazed at her, appearing extremely pleased with himself. "I finally won you over. Holy shit."

"Don't fuck it up," she said, holding up a finger. "I still expect you to do full parent duty from here on out."

"If I don't will you punish me?" he asked, waggling his brows.

"Let's just say, if you *do*, I *might* be open to ordering more sexy outfits."

"Woman, you just made my year. Hell, I think you just made my life."

Eventually, she finished her wine and Peter drove them home. When they'd paid Kara and turned off all the lights, she slipped her hand into his and led him upstairs.

"Are we going to finally bang in your bed?" he asked, sliding his arms around her waist as they entered her room.

"If I don't pass out first," she said, feeling so free as she stood on the precipice of the next phase of her life with the man she adored. "Better hurry."

Lifting her, he silenced her tiny squeal with his mouth before carrying her to bed and christening it properly and thoroughly.

Chapter 19

Peter began the move, loving how excited the boys were. They each showed him their special spots around the house, proving he was, indeed, becoming part of their small-knit group. It made him feel extremely special and he took it very seriously.

Sebastian's favorite spot was under the front porch. As it turned out, there was a small gap one could crawl through that opened up to a pretty cool fort he'd built. He stored action figures and little trinkets there, and showed them to Peter one day as he sat in the cramped space.

"See?" Sebastian asked, holding up a dirty coin. "Ashlyn gave it to me and said it might have been Sally Pickens'. We'll never know for sure though."

Peter pursed his lips, remembering when Ashlyn had purchased the old coins at the street fair and thought they'd make a cute gift for the boys. The Sally Pickens tie-in was a nice touch. "That's really cool, buddy. Any update on the buried treasure behind her house?"

"No, but we're going to dig again next weekend. Mom says we need to do it before it gets cold since August is almost over and we're going back to school soon."

"Are you excited to go back?"

"Yeah. I had to make up all the tests and stuff I missed at the end of last year online and that was annoying. But Mom said she didn't want me to be held back so I did it."

"We're two peas in a pod, kid. I think we're both pretty stubborn but would do anything to see your mom smile."

Nodding, he shrugged. "It was pretty easy and I knew if I did it, she wouldn't yell at me."

"Smart move."

Peter hung out with him until his back began to ache in the cramped space. Heading inside to start unpacking the boxes he'd brought over, he began stuffing his clothing into the drawers Carrie had assigned him in the dresser. After dinner, she walked into the room with the laundry basket against her hip.

"Is there some reason why I get one closet rack and you get the other two?"

"You're lucky I gave you one, buddy," she said, folding the clothes as she sat atop the bed. "I moved a bunch of stuff to the guest bedroom closet but I'm not happy about it. Hope the sacrifice is worth it."

Placing his hand over his heart, he fell to the bed. "Woman, you wound me."

Her laugh surrounded him as she tucked two socks into a ball. "We haven't lived together since you were in college. Well, you technically still lived with your mom but you stayed over all the time. Anyway, it was a long time ago. Think we'll get tired of each other?"

"No freaking way," he said, picking up one of the shirts in the basket and folding it. "We're both much easier to get along with now that we're older and less dramatic."

Breathing a laugh, she shrugged. "Or maybe we're more set in our ways."

"You're definitely a little demon when you wake up in the morning. I forgot how scary you are before your first cup of coffee."

"Ha. Ha," she said, lodging a sock roll at his head. "I just need a routine and some quiet in the morning. You never understood that."

"Maybe you'll be more amenable if I wake you up with sex every day," he said, crawling over the bed and dislodging the perfect piles of clothing she'd assembled.

"Peter!" she scolded, pushing him away. "You're messing up the laundry. Damn it."

"I'm sorry," he mumbled into the skin of her neck as he drew her close. Kicking the basket and most of the piles to the floor, he flipped her to lie on her back as he loomed over her. "Oops."

"You're like one of the kids," she said, playfully shoving him. "Get off me or you're doing the next three batches of laundry."

"Worth it." Lowering his lips to hers, he slid his hand beneath the waistband of her shorts. Running his fingers over the tiny patch of hair that covered her mound, he grazed his lips over hers. "I'm so happy to be here, honey. I missed being here all the time."

"Well, you're in it now, laundry duty and all," she said, sliding her arms around his neck. "Now that you're here, might as well take advantage."

Never one to squander and opportunity, he listened to his lover, ensuring she forgot all about the damn laundry.

The next morning, once Carrie had her coffee and was coherent, they prepped the boys and loaded into the SUV to head to the lake. It was about a twenty-minute drive away and they'd decided to spend the day there since the kids would be returning to school after Labor Day. Peter was determined to teach them to fish since it was a pastime he enjoyed. Shortly after the lesson began, he realized teaching an eight and ten-year-old anything was pretty much a nightmare.

"It's wiggling," Charlie said, holding up the worm. "I don't want to kill him."

"It's all part of the food chain, kid. We'll catch what we eat and your mom can cook them so they're really yummy. If we eat them, the worm will have valiantly died for the cause."

"Mom's not cooking fish," Carrie called from her seat atop the blanket a few feet away, her eyes never leaving the tablet as she read a book. "If Peter doesn't want the worm to suffer, he's going to have to catch and release or catch and cook."

"You're a real team player there, Care Bear," he mocked as she held up her fist, backside facing him. He knew she only kept the middle finger down because the boys were watching. "Okay, fine, I'll contemplate cooking the fish. Let's try and catch some."

The boys were terrible at casting, each of them landing in every possible spot except the water. Sebastian eventually became frustrated and complained he wanted to play his handheld video game.

"Let's try a little while longer before we give up on nature," Peter said, positioning the pole in the boy's hand. "Okay, give it a go."

Sebastian slung the line from behind his shoulder out to the water and the hook landed on a small piece of driftwood. He reeled it in as Charlie exclaimed, "You caught something!"

"Not really the intended target, but we'll focus on the positives," Peter said, grimacing.

Charlie ended up getting the hang of it and finally got a nibble on his hook. The pole jerked in his hand and he looked at Peter, eyes wide. "What do I do?"

"Reel him in," Peter said, placing his hand over Charlie's and helping him rotate. "You've got it. Keep going!"

The fish slid onto the sand, flopping as Charlie ran toward it, crouching down. "It's so gross!"

"Just a little fish," Peter said, grabbing the flailing animal and holding it tight. "Since your Mom's not up for cooking, I say we throw him back. You slide the hook out like this." Removing the hook, he showed Charlie as he looked on with rapt attention.

"Cool," he breathed.

"Okay, now we throw him back in. Hold out your hands and grip him tight when I hand him over."

Charlie took the fish and walked to the edge of the water.

"Toss it back in!" Peter yelled.

Throwing with both arms, he threw the fish back into the lake.

"Well done! You caught your first fish. I'm so proud of you, buddy!" Giving him a high five, he turned and waved Sebastian over. "You're next. Let's get a new worm on your hook."

"This is stupid," Sebastian said, kicking the ground. "Can I sit with Mom?"

Peter felt his heart deflate in his chest. Something about the kid's rejection rankled him. "Sure, if you want to."

Sebastian headed over to sit with Carrie while Charlie stared up at Peter with anticipation. "Can I try to catch another one?"

"Sure thing. Let's do it."

Charlie ended up catching and releasing two more fish before they all sat on the blanket and Carrie opened the picnic basket. Once their hands had been thoroughly wiped down with the antibacterial wipes she always carried, they dug into the sandwiches and snacks she'd made. After lunch, the boys wanted to swim, so Peter divested his shirt and lay on the blanket, crossing his hands behind his head to soak up some rays.

"Your scar healed nicely," Carrie said, glancing at his abdomen. "Sebastian's did too, thank goodness. He thinks it's cool you both have matching scars."

"I'm so glad his recovery was smoother than mine. His side effects from the immunosuppressant medication don't seem to be that bad either."

"Nope. He's a champ. He complains of nausea sometimes after he takes it but other than that, we've been really lucky."

Peter listened to the boys splashing in the water, bummed Sebastian hadn't enjoyed fishing as he'd hoped.

"Sebastian's at an age," Carrie said, closing the picnic basket after loading the remnants of their picnic inside. "He's not an easy child at the moment. I spoke to his pediatrician about it and he says he should grow out of it over time. Jeff leaving was hard and sometimes I wonder if I should take him to see a child psychologist."

"What did the pediatrician say about that?" Peter asked.

"He said to give it some time and if I don't see a change after he turns eleven, it might be best to take him to see someone. He also told me kids are difficult and cranky and I needed to go easy on myself. It's good advice to remember so I'm passing it on to you."

"I guess it's obvious I'm devastated he hates fishing. I figured he'd love it since I do."

"He doesn't seem to really love anything but video games and sports these days, so I let him focus on those as long as he does his chores and doesn't misbehave."

"I worry about him having my issues," he said, absently staring at the boys as they swam.

"About him being an addict?"

Peter nodded. "I was just like him as a kid. You remember. Angry and annoyed at everything."

"Honestly, he's not half as bad as you were."

He glowered, squinting at her as her head blocked out the sun.

"Don't give me that look. You were a little shit. And then you grew into a big shit. I wonder why I fell in love with you in the first place."

Sliding his hand over her thigh, he squeezed. "You love that I was a bad boy. I think it twisted your preacher-girl panties."

"In your dreams," she said, squishing her nose. "I should've dated Ryan Mills when he asked me out in ninth grade. Everything would've been so different. I could've been Mrs. Ryan Mills and had a bunch of little Ryans running around."

"Are you trying to make me hate you? Is this about the closet? You can have the rack back. I don't need clothes anyway."

Laughing, she lay on her side and rested her head on her hand as her elbow dug into the blanket. "Maybe I liked that you were a bit of a rebel," she said, tracing her hand over his pec. "And you were always so damn hot. It wasn't fair. My teenage hormone-filled body never stood a chance."

Chuckling, he tucked a curl behind her ear. Her eyes were so clear as they sparkled in the mid-day sun. "I don't want him to be an addict, Carrie. I hope I didn't saddle him with that. It's a terrible burden."

"Hey," she said, stroking his jaw. "It is what it is, Peter. He's so much like you, it's scary sometimes. We just have to do our best and foster open communication. Worrying about it is futile. Day by day, right? Isn't that what you learn in AA?"

"Among other things. At least I know the signs. I'll do everything in my power to prevent him from making my mistakes."

"We can't stop them from making mistakes," she said with a gentle smile. "That's one of the hardest lessons of parenting. They have to make them so they can learn their own lessons. It would be so much easier if we could learn for them but it doesn't work that way."

"Damn. This whole parenting thing is complex as hell. If we do end up having a girl, I'm declaring at birth she can't date until she's twenty. I know exactly what teenage boys are thinking and we'll just have to build her a nice bunker to stay in until I'm senile and can't comprehend she's having sex."

"*You* tried to have sex with me when we were fifteen."

"Exactly. Hence, the bunker."

Snickering, she bit her lip. "You've brought this up a few times. You really want to have a baby? That's a whole other level of intense, Peter."

"I want to experience the entire journey with you, honey," he said, cupping her jaw. "After rehab, I thought about everything I threw away. I realized how much I regretted not having kids with you and never dreamed I'd get the chance. Do you want to have more?"

Chewing her lip, she nodded. "Yes. Seeing Ashlyn pregnant reminds me of how much I adored having little babies. Every milestone is so cute and reaffirms how precious life is."

"Let's start trying before I go bald and you won't make love to me because I remind you of Sam the organ player from church."

Throwing back her head, she broke into melodious laughter. "Sam was very sweet and I liked his bald head."

"Sweet enough to bang? I remember him smelling like stale peppermints."

"You're ridiculous," she said, swatting his shoulder. Studying him, she contemplated. "All right," she finally said, emotion swimming in her green eyes. "I'll make an appointment to get the IUD removed. Holy shit. This is next level, Peter. Are you sure?"

"Yes," he whispered, taken by the moment.

Her smile was breathtaking as she snuggled into his side and rested her head on his chest. The boys played in the water until she remarked they must be getting shriveled. Grabbing two towels, she strolled over and helped them dry as Peter watched from the shore.

As they drove home, Peter laced his fingers through Carrie's as the boys slept in the back seat.

"They're out cold," he whispered.

"Let's leave it that way," she said, lifting her finger over her lips.

Squeezing her hand, he marveled at how much his life had changed in a matter of months...and at how incredibly lucky he was to be a part of their tight-knit family.

Chapter 20

♥

Carrie woke up the morning of her fortieth birthday angry as a hornet. Even though things had been going pretty well, she wasn't thrilled at the milestone, especially when Peter was chipper as a damn teenager.

"Good morning, sleeping beauty," he said, thrusting a paper cup in her face labeled *Care Bear*. "It's extra strong since we have a full day ahead of us."

"I told you I didn't want anything special," she said, burying her face in the pillow and waving him away. "Just let me sleep. That's the best present you could give me."

"The boys want to celebrate you," he said, poking her shoulder. "Come on. They're excited to go on the hike."

Groaning, she sat up and grabbed the coffee, scowling as she sipped. "How do you always have so much energy in the morning? It's baffling."

"I've always been that way. Don't ask me. You should've seen me when I was doing coke. I was unstoppable."

"No thanks," she muttered.

"Are you hungry?"

"I guess. I'll make us some omelets. Give me a minute to get dressed."

"Thanks, honey. See you downstairs." Whistling as he walked away, she rolled her eyes, wondering how long she could lie back down and sleep before he returned. Deciding it wasn't worth the effort, she took another huge swig and dressed in sweats before throwing her hair in a bun.

Trailing downstairs, she entered the kitchen, eyes narrowing as she smelled something cooking. Glancing toward the stove, she broke into a huge smile.

"Happy birthday, Mom!" the boys said, holding signs that read *Happy Birthday* while Peter stood behind them, flipping pancakes.

"You guys didn't have to do this," she said as tears welled in her eyes.

"Peter said we need to make you feel special since you're old," Sebastian said, running over and hugging her around the waist.

"But you're still really pretty, Mom," Charlie said, throwing his arms around her too.

"What I *said* is that it's your fortieth birthday and that's really special," Peter said, scrunching his nose at the boys as he smiled over his shoulder, "but I guess that does mean old to a certain audience."

Squeezing the boys, she disentangled and approached Peter. Sliding her arms around his waist, she kissed the back of his neck. "You're cooking pancakes."

"Yep. Half of them aren't even burnt and might actually be edible."

Taking pity on him, she took the spatula and flipped a few over. "They look great. Thank you. Oh, and I see we have sausage too."

"Don't think I can mess that up. I am a pretty good griller, at least." He used a fork to move the links around the pan. "Go on and sit with the boys. I'll bring everything over when it's ready."

The breakfast was fantastic, spurring Carrie to joke that Peter had to cook every morning now that she knew he had the skill. The boys laughed as he held up his napkin and hid behind it, attempting to hide from her proclamation. Eventually, they finished up and headed out for a hike at the nearby park.

As they strolled along the wide path, she held Peter's hand while the boys ran along in front of them, stopping every few minutes to look at different bugs and flowers.

"This is a really nice day," she said, giving him a soft grin.

"It is. I'm having fun."

"Me too. I'm excited to try the fancy new restaurant with Scott and Ashlyn tonight. Thanks for making the reservation."

"Sure. Gotta wine and dine you on your birthday. Maybe I'll get lucky and you'll break out the nurse outfit again."

"Oh, buddy, we're way past sexy nurse. I think pancakes and sausage might have earned you sexy teacher. And you'll definitely need *a lot* of instruction."

He tugged her hand, causing her to halt, and slid his arm around her waist. Drawing her into his body, he murmured, "Are you trying to make me drag you into the woods and ravish you? Because I'll do it."

"Later," she said, placing a sweet kiss on his lips. "But you're definitely getting laid tonight."

Squeezing her ass, he gave a low growl. "I might have to fuck you before we go to dinner."

"If the boys get lost in the new video game, we might be able to convince them we're folding laundry upstairs for twenty minutes...with the door closed...and locked."

Laughing, he chucked his brows. "Lots of laundry to do. I'm hammering that message home, for sure."

"Good luck. They're always curious when I lock the door."

His brows drew together. "How often do you lock the door?"

"Before you moved in? Three times a week, minimum. They were very special times spent with my trusty vibrator."

"Your vibrator can join us during laundry too."

Chuckling, she lifted to her toes and whispered in his ear. "If you're lucky."

"Boys! Let's hike for another half hour then we need to get home to do laundry. Lots of laundry."

The boys yelled, "Okay!" as Carrie threw back her head and broke into joyful laughter.

"You're incorrigible."

"Don't forget it." Clutching her hand, they eventually finished the hike and headed home.

After an extremely intense *laundry* session in the bedroom, Carrie rested a bit before getting ready for dinner. She hadn't dressed up in so long and wanted to knock Peter's socks off, especially since she'd reached the four-decade milestone. Good grief, where had the years gone? As she applied makeup in the bathroom mirror, she reflected on all the peaks and valleys of her life thus far.

Would the next few decades be more even-keeled with less dramatic ebbs and flows? She wasn't certain but knew she hadn't felt so balanced in years. Yes, it had to do with Peter and his unwavering desire to be a part of her and the boys' lives. But, more so, it stemmed from the fact she'd grown into her confidence and strength. She'd held her ground when Peter pushed, understanding they both needed to truly comprehend the significance of building a life together.

In her youth, she might not have been as resolute but she was proud of her will and resolve, firmly believing it would lead to a stronger constitution for their combined family. By challenging Peter, and herself, she set them up for future success. Excited for everything they would build together, she finished her makeup and headed to the closet to don the new dress she'd purchased last week.

Peter walked into the bedroom as she was attempting to zip up the back.

"Can you help me? I can't reach my middle back."

He stood frozen, eyes raking over her in the tight forest green dress.

"Peter?"

"Holy shit," he breathed, slowly approaching and gliding a finger across the top of her breasts. "This is so sexy."

"It's kind of low cut but I figured why the hell not? I think I look pretty good."

"You look amazing," he said, sliding his palms over her hips. "I'm feeling some weird Neanderthal possessive vibes here. Should I drag you by the hair and lock you away so no one else can see you?"

Chuckling, she turned and lifted her hair so he could access the zipper. "Not if you want to live. I'd tamp down the urges."

"Fuck, Carrie," he said, zipping the dress before placing a soft kiss on her shoulder. "How did I ever leave you? Was I blind?"

"No," she said, turning and sliding her arms around his neck. "You were just young and stupid. We both were."

"Let's get this dinner over with because I'm going to rip this thing off when we get home."

"It cost two hundred dollars so you'll do no such thing. You can drag it off me. Slowly. Got it?"

"Yes, ma'am," he said, nipping the finger she pointed at him. "Let's go."

"Let me pack my clutch. Go downstairs and meet Kara. She should be here soon." When he pulled the door open, she called his name.

"Yeah?" he asked, turning.

"You look really nice too," she said, noting how handsome he was in his slacks, freshly pressed collared shirt and blazer.

"Thanks, honey. See you downstairs."

As they drove to the restaurant, which was located a block behind Main Street, Peter held her hand, their fingers laced in her lap, as he drove. A sense of contentment washed over Carrie as tears swam in her eyes. She'd lived through so much heartache, most recently with the divorce, and had always fought her battles alone. Finally, after all this time, she had a partner. How strange.

"Are you already crying?" Peter teased, squeezing her hand. "I'm sure the food's not that bad."

"Oh, stop," she said, playfully swatting his shoulder. "I'm just happy. I thought forty would be awful but it's actually pretty awesome. I'm excited to try this place. It has great reviews."

They valeted the car and Peter led the way as Carrie noticed how dim the restaurant was. Since it was the fanciest new restaurant in Ardor Creek, she figured it must be some sort of new-wave atmosphere. Stepping inside, she gasped as light flooded the room.

"Surprise!"

Covering her heart with her hand, Carrie observed the crowd of people, noticing Ashlyn and Scott, Terry and her husband, Chad Hanson, the mayor, with what looked to be his current flame, and so many more. Gazing up at Peter, she beamed.

"Did you do this?"

"Uh, yeah," he said, giving her a goofy grin. "Forty is a big deal, Care Bear. We all wanted to show up for you."

"Thank you," she whispered, heart pounding in her chest as Ashlyn approached.

"Happy birthday!" she exclaimed, hugging her. "Are you surprised?"

"So surprised. I can't believe you guys did this."

"You do so much for everyone else and your boys. We wanted to treat you for once. Come on, let's mingle. Peter booked the Ardor Boys so we can dance after dinner," Ashlyn said, referring to the local band that was set up in the back of the large room.

Carrie shot Peter one last smile before being dragged around the room into fervent embraces and well wishes. Drinks were thrust into her hand whenever her current one was low and, eventually, she sat down to a fantastic family-style dinner full of luscious appetizers, pasta, and birthday cake for dessert. The band played a raucous version of "Happy Birthday to You" as the crowd joined in and sang along.

"Well, you might not need any help busting me out of this dress," Carrie said, rubbing her stomach as she grinned at Peter after finishing the large piece of cake. "I think it's about to burst."

Leaning over, he whispered in her ear, "Anything that makes that dress fall off is fine with me. I can't stop staring at you."

"You're already getting laid," she said, nipping his lips. "You don't have to pour it on."

Chuckling, he stood and extended his hand. "Dance with me."

He led her onto the wooden dance floor as the band played a sultry George Michael song in the background. Resting her cheek on his shoulder, she relaxed as his strong arm surrounded her waist, the other hand holding hers as they swayed.

"Maybe this will make up for prom when I got wasted and puked in the back of your hatchback."

"God, it was everywhere," she said, wrinkling her nose. "I barely saw you that night. I remember being so pissed."

"I remember begging for an inordinately long period of time before you let me touch you under your panties again."

Laughing, she nodded. "Yep. I made you work for it."

Placing a tender kiss on her forehead, he drew her into his frame until they almost melded. "But you eventually forgave me."

"What can I say? You're always so cute when you apologize."

His deep laugh surrounded them as the song ended. The band broke into a Michael Jackson song and Ashlyn approached, grabbing Carrie's wrist.

"Oh, we're dancing to this one. I don't care that I might topple over," she said, pointing to her abdomen. "Come on, Carrie."

They danced late into the night, Carrie's heart full from all the love bestowed upon her by her friends, many whom she'd known her whole life. Once the party wound down, and they loaded all of Carrie's gifts in the car, Peter drove them home.

"You got a lot of wine," he said, gesturing with his head to the backseat.

"And lots of gift cards. Can't wait to go shopping. It's been a while since I had a spree at the mall. People didn't have to buy me gifts but I definitely appreciate it."

Deciding to unpack the car tomorrow, they paid Kara and turned off the lights before heading upstairs. After checking to ensure both boys were sleeping soundly, they entered the bedroom, anticipation buzzing in Carrie's veins.

Peter threw his sport coat over the chair in the corner and trailed toward her as she stood by the bed. His full lips curved into a sexy smile as he brushed her body with his.

"I'm going to make you scream tonight, honey," he said, his tone low as he inserted a finger between her breasts. Dragging it over her flushed skin, he ran his fingernail over her nipple as she whimpered. Tugging the dress, he bared her breast, the puckered bud tight and ruddy as it called to him.

"You teased me all night with this fucking dress," he whispered, cupping her breast and lifting it. "I might need to punish you."

Ragged breaths were her only answer as he lowered his head and murmured against her nipple. "You little tease. You love driving me crazy."

Thrusting her fingers in his hair, she drew him close. "*Peter...*"

"Mmm..." he moaned, extending his tongue and flicking the sensitive bud. "Fuck, you taste so good." Opening his mouth, he sucked her inside as her head fell back while she clutched his hair.

He nibbled and licked, causing her body to quiver, before wrenching the fabric from her other breast and repeating the lascivious ministrations. Clamping the nub with his teeth, he tugged, sending jolts of pleasure through her frame. Feeling her knees start to buckle, she fell limp in his arms.

"Unzip my dress," she commanded, reaching behind her and flailing for the zipper. "*Please...*"

Growling with desire, his broad hands gripped her waist and turned her to face the bed. After sliding the zipper down, he pulled the dress from her body and gently pushed her to lay across the bed.

"These lacy panties are so hot," he said, gripping the band of her thong and pulling it tight into her wet folds, causing her to whimper into the comforter as her cheek rested on the bed. "I want to rip them off."

"Do it," she moaned, bracing when his grip tightened. The sound of ripping fabric reverberated in the room as the flimsy garment was torn from her body.

Peter inhaled, the sound full and deep as he smoothed his palms over the mounds of her ass. Pulling them apart, he elicited a guttural sound before sliding his fingers over her tiny puckered hole to the wet flesh beneath.

"Was your pussy wet like this all night?" he asked, gliding his finger over her drenched opening. "Just waiting for me to take you when we got home?"

Carrie whimpered, pushing against his hand.

"Tell me," he commanded, slapping her ass before soothing the sting with his palm. "Were you dripping for me tonight, honey?"

"Yes," she cried, her voice hoarse and breathy. "Fuck me..."

"Soon, honey," he said, slapping her other ass cheek before smoothing away the tiny pricks of pain. "Do you want it hard?"

"Yessss..."

Hissing out a breath, he pinched her clit and Carrie saw stars. He flicked the sensitive bud, back and forth, as she squirmed. Cursing, he removed his hand and she heard the rustle of clothes being ripped off.

The tip of his cock lodged against her wet folds, sliding through her essence. Leaning over, he gripped her thick hair and tugged her head back.

"Is this what you want?" he murmured against her ear, gliding his cock over her deepest place.

"Oh, god, yes! Damn it, Peter. Stop teasing me."

"Relax and open up for me, honey," he whispered, aligning his shaft with her opening.

Exhaling, she released every bit of tension in her straining body, preparing for his invasion. He slammed inside her taut channel, impaling her as he groaned in her ear. His fist tightened in her hair, magnifying the pleasure, and she gave over to him, body and soul.

"There's that hot, tight pussy you've been teasing me with all night," he murmured, bucking as her body bowed. "Yeah, sweetheart, take me deep. *Fuck...*"

"Harder," she demanded, pushing against him as his hips worked their furious pace.

He cupped her mound, stimulating her clit as he fucked her from behind. His other hand was still lodged in her hair as he spoke low and sexy in her ear. "I never dreamed I'd be able to fuck you like this again, Carrie. You feel so good, honey."

The head of his cock roused nerves so deep inside she felt weightless. Reaching behind, she gripped his hair, pulling his face into hers. "I gave up... I never thought you'd want this life—"

"I'm here," he gritted, slamming his body into hers.

"I know."

"I *love you*."

Burying her face in the soft comforter, she couldn't fathom saying it back. Not when he was driving her insane with lust and her body was on fire.

"Goddammit, Carrie. Are you ever going to say it back?"

Whimpering, she dug farther into the bed.

Sounds of slapping flesh echoed off the walls from their sweat-soaked bodies. His fingers worked magic on her clit as the head of his cock stimulated the tiny bundle of nerves so deep within.

"I need to know you love me, honey. *Fuck*...I'm going to come..."

Tossing her head back on his shoulder, her body exploded as the orgasm took hold. Racked with tremors, her muscles turned to jelly as he pistoned inside her, the movements frenzied and erratic. Muttering unintelligible words in her ear, his body jerked as he began to climax, jets of release spurting from his shaft as he clutched her tight. Carrie pushed into his body, wanting to feel every inch of his skin as he unleashed his wet release inside her quivering frame. His hips surged against her ass, emptying every last pulsing drop until they both collapsed in a heap of heaving lungs and tingling bodies. Unable to hear anything over the buzzing in her ears, she closed her eyes, hoping it would help amplify the words he was droning in her ear.

"Huh?" she mumbled against the mattress.

"Happy birthday, old lady." His chest vibrated with laughter as he bit the shell of her ear.

"Screw you," she mumbled.

"Uh, yeah, not for a while. You sucked me dry, honey. Holy shit. I'm spent." Sliding his arm between her breasts, he pulled her close, spooning her as they recovered. His palm rested above her pounding heart and she snuggled into him, waiting for her heartbeat to return to normal.

"You used to spank me like that when we began experimenting after I moved into my apartment."

"Mmm-hmm," he said, nuzzling her neck. "I think you like it."

"I love it."

"Noted." Running his thumb over the soft skin above her breasts, he burrowed into her. After a while, his deep baritone filtered through her frame. "I need you to say it back, honey. If you can't, you need to tell me why."

Exhaling, she closed her eyes. His pain was palpable and she hated causing it. "I'm so scared, Peter."

"Still?" he asked, the strokes of his thumb so soothing. "I'm trying so hard—"

"I know," she said, shaking her head. "But part of me is still terrified. I'm sorry if that hurts. I don't want to hurt you. You're doing everything right but it's only been a few months. Our past has been comprised of so many amazing moments followed by so much pain. The words are the last thing I have left to give."

Sighing, he nodded against her neck. "Okay, honey. I guess I squandered all the times you said them freely. I should've realized how precious they were then."

"We just need to settle into this. Let me settle in in my own way, okay?"

"Okay." Placing a kiss on her head, he shifted. "In the meantime, I'm slipping all over the place. We made a mess."

Snickering, she willed her body to move and sat up. Extending her hand, she dragged him from the mattress so they could brush their teeth and prep for bed. Once under the covers, her in a tank and shorts and him in boxers in case the kids needed something, he drew her close.

"Love you, honey," he said, placing a peck on her forehead as she rested her cheek on his chest. "Hope you had a happy birthday."

"Thank you, Peter," she said, emotion making her voice thick. "You made me feel so special."

"How long has it been since someone went out of their way for you?" he asked, gently stroking her arm.

Eyebrows drawing together, she pondered. "I don't know. I like doing things for other people and the boys aren't really old enough to realize how much it would mean if they took the time to do things for me."

"Exactly. That's going to change. I'm going to teach these kids how lucky they are to have you. That's going to include a lot of breakfasts in bed and making-mom-feel-special time."

"Aw," she said, squeezing him. "That's sweet, but I enjoy taking care of them. They're my babies."

"That's great but they need to realize how good they have it. Take it from the kid of a shithead parent, these boys are extremely lucky."

"I'm glad you think I'm a good mom," she said, feeling herself drift as her eyelids drooped. "I try so hard and it's exhausting."

"You're not alone anymore, Carrie. One day, you'll accept I'm here to stay."

"One day."

Darkness set in as she soaked in the warmth of his embrace. Hours later, she lifted her lids to find Charlie standing beside the bed. They'd unlocked the door after their steamy tryst and she rolled over to face him.

"Hey, baby," she whispered, stroking his cheek. "Did you have a nightmare?"

Shaking his head, he clutched Bear. "There's a ghost in my room. She's friends with Sally Pickens. She's nice but it scared me."

"Oh, that does sound scary," she said, reaching for him. Dragging him into bed, she snuggled him close and pulled up the covers. "We'll just sleep in here tonight and let the ghost be comfortable in your bed for one night only, okay? Tomorrow, we'll tell her she needs to find another bed to sleep in."

"Okay," he said, nuzzling into her as he gripped Bear tight.

Peter's arm snaked over both of them as he snuggled into her back. "You guys okay?" he asked sleepily.

"We're good. Charlie just has a ghost in his room. She's going to go back home tomorrow."

"Sounds good. I'll talk to her tomorrow and tell her you need your room back. Night, guys."

"Night, Peter. Love you," Charlie said.

Tears welled in Carrie's eyes as Peter's arm tightened around them.

"Love you too, buddy."

Surrounded by her sweet men, Carrie fell into a deep slumber.

Chapter 21

♥

Mid-September arrived, leaving a whirlwind of activity in its wake. The boys returned to school and Peter settled into the new office Scott built. The space was perfect and Peter loved working there since Carrie was stationed only yards away. Several times a day, he would skulk to her desk, located by the entrance, and proceed to drive her crazy as she tried to work. She would glare at him in frustration as she spoke into the headset to Scott's clients and then berate him once she hung up the phone.

The woman could feign all she wanted but Peter knew the truth: she was mad for him.

The Carrie he'd come to know when he'd returned to Ardor Creek was all but gone. That weary soul—hardened and battered by a brutal divorce and several failures at love—had been replaced by a stronger and fiercer Carrie Longwood. Peter had loved her when she was shattered and disillusioned. Now, she'd grown into someone so magnificent, she'd stolen his soul. For the first time in their extensive, arduous relationship, Peter wasn't the one with the power to leave. Carrie controlled the balance and he was powerless to do anything but let her steer ahead and hope she didn't decide he wasn't worthy of being part of her family.

Of course, a step toward cementing that was ensuring he married her as soon as possible. Peter understood this would solidify something in her still-trepidatious nature. The infuriating women still hadn't uttered the three little words he so vehemently craved and he understood they symbolized something deep and unwavering for her. Vowing to be patient, he began to plot the steps toward making her his wife.

His plan took a fortuitous turn when his cell rang one day in late-September. Smiling at the caller ID, he lifted it to his ear.

"Bradley Whitford. I thought you drowned the night you disappeared from the yacht when we had that massive bender with Richard Branson."

A deep chuckle reverberated through the phone. "I can't believe you even remember that night. We were wasted as shit."

"Par for the course back then," Peter said, leaning back in his chair and rubbing his neck. "What's up? Haven't heard from you in years. Are you still at the firm?"

"Yep. I'm a senior partner now and making a shit ton of money I probably don't deserve, but that's the financial world for you. You still stuck in the sticks doing grandma's taxes?"

"Sure am," Peter said, laughing. "I know it sounds awful but it's actually been great. Really great recently since I reconnected with my high school flame."

"The redhead you used to always talk about?"

"That's the one. She's decided to give me another chance and I'm trying like hell not to blow it."

"Good for you, man. I'm happy for you. I'm still screwing my way through the city. Just can't seem to find the urge to settle down."

"Hey, we're all where we need to be. I've been sober for three years and have never felt better."

"That's inspiring, man. I might reach out to you when I'm ready to turn the page. In the meantime, I'm calling you with a lead, of sorts."

Peter's eyebrows drew together. "Okay."

"One of our whale investors just bought three hundred acres near Scranton and intends to build a golf course. He wants the firm to recommend someone local to personally manage the finances and accounting for the venture. Your name came up in the board meeting this morning and we think you'd be perfect."

"Wow. I can't believe no one else snatched it up."

"Not to be a dick, but none of us have any desire to hang out near Scranton all the time. Sorry, buddy."

"Okay, okay," Peter said, grinning. "It's not *that* bad." Gears shifted and turned in his brain as he contemplated. "What would it entail?"

"You'd have to come into the city at first to solidify everything. You remember the drill. Wining and dining until the investor feels comfortable with you. You always were a charmer so I don't anticipate it being too difficult to get him on board."

Rubbing his forehead, Peter pondered.

"Okay," he finally said, sitting up straighter. "I'm interested, especially since the previously mentioned redhead has two boys. I have to think about things like college funds and sports team costs now. That stuff isn't cheap."

"Just a second. I have to process this new domesticated version of Peter Stratford."

"Ha. Ha. Don't knock it 'til you try it, dude. The sex is better than ever and the kids are adorable. I'm like a pig in shit."

"Well, hot damn. I'm glad you're interested. We're taking Larry—that's the investor—out to dinner tomorrow night. It will be a late night since he has a proclivity for expensive scotch and even more expensive women."

"Obviously, I won't partake in any of that," Peter droned.

"Of course not, but you still have to schmooze. You should probably get a hotel."

Peter's heart began to pound as he imagined Carrie's reaction to the news he was going to spend the night in the city surrounded by the vices of his old life. Deciding he needed to speak to her first, he relayed that sentiment to Bradley.

"No prob, man. Talk to your old lady but I need to know by nine o'clock tonight. If you're not able to dedicate the time to securing this client, we'll need to find someone else."

"I'll talk to her at dinner tonight. You'll hear from me before nine. In the meantime, send over everything you've compiled on the deal so I can crunch the numbers and figure out exactly how much this would bring in. I'll text you my email address. Thanks for thinking of me for this, Brad. I really appreciate it."

"No sweat. You were the best broker the firm had. It hurt to see you leave us for Mayberry."

"Had to save my damn life, man. I used to miss city life but I honestly haven't thought about it in a while. Guess I'm finally old and settled down."

"Better you than me. Call me when you have an answer. Talk soon."

Sighing, Peter ran his hand through his hair, wondering how many cracks the opportunity would open in Carrie's fragile tether of trust. Realizing there was only one way to find out, he mentally prepared to have the discussion with her.

Later that evening, as they finished dinner at the round kitchen table, Carrie's gaze kept sliding to Peter. His energy was different—more excited somehow—and she wondered what had spurred the change. Once the boys were settled into the living room and she'd packed the leftovers, she poured a glass of wine and sat down at the table where he was tinkering on his laptop.

"Okay," she said, reaching over and closing the laptop. "Something's up. Might as well get it out in the open."

"I should be used to your mindreading skills by now," he said, grinning as he threaded his fingers behind his head.

"You should be. So, what's up? If it's about helping Ashlyn with the upcoming haunted homes tours, I'm all for it. Can't believe it will be October soon. Where did the year go?"

"I'm excited to help her and I think the boys will love being included. But it's about something else."

"Okay," she said, curious as she sipped the wine.

"I got a call from one of my old partners in the city today. He had this really interesting proposition." Carrie listened as he told her about the investor, his tone enthusiastic as he detailed the venture.

"It sounds like a great opportunity," she said when he finished.

"It is. Clients like this are few and far between. Brad emailed me some information on the investor, the land he bought, and the development plans for the golf course. I could make more on this one client than all my other local accounting clients combined."

"I didn't realize you were looking to make more. Once your Mom's house closes we'll get a bump in savings and you're already making six figures."

"I guess I just thought about the boys," he said, shrugging. "What if they want to go to an Ivy League school or, hell, any top-notch school for that matter? It doesn't hurt to supplement our income. Plus, Sebastian's surgery was expensive and it will help pay off the loan you took out to pay for the deductible and expenses."

Carrie's eyes darted between his. "This reminds me of the old Peter who always wanted more. The next shiny object. Are you worried it will trigger the addict inside?"

His brow furrowed. "Not in the least. It's a local job, Carrie. I would only have to go to the city in the beginning."

Dread, heavy and sticky, pervaded her veins. For some reason, the thought of Peter spending time in the city represented every single fear she had about him eventually leaving her again.

"Hey," he said, leaning forward and encircling her wrist. "I can read you pretty well too, you know? You're freaking out and I need you to take a deep breath. This isn't the past. It's a new opportunity for us that we'd be stupid to not consider."

"How long?" she asked, swallowing thickly.

"What?"

"How long would you have to go to the city to secure the client?"

"I'm not sure," he said, releasing her wrist and rubbing his chin. "The first acquisition dinner is tomorrow night. After that, I'd have to go in at least four or five more times, minimum, I think. I'd need to have some day meetings at the firm and some additional dinners to finalize everything."

"And after that, everything would be local?"

He nodded. "Once the contracts are finalized, I would only meet with him out here. I'm not servicing anything but the golf course. The firm will still manage all of his assets in the city."

Inhaling a deep breath, Carrie chewed her lip. "What happens at these 'dinners'?" she made quotation marks with her hands. "Drinking, drugs, and hookers?"

"Yes," he said, gaze cemented to hers. "I don't want to lie to you. It's just the way it's done with these rich clients."

"And you think you'll just be able to wave good night while they continue and partake?"

"I do," he said with a tilt of his head. "I'm over that shit, Carrie. I know it's hard for you to believe but I like living. That lifestyle almost killed me. I'm resolved to wine and dine him while making clear I have a wife and kids at home and don't have any interest in anything else."

The words spurred a smile. "I'm not your wife."

"So, let's get married," he said, flashing his perfect white teeth. "I'm ready. I was waiting to ask you until we'd settled in a bit more but I'll marry you right now, honey."

"I was hoping for a proposal that was a *tad* more romantic," she teased.

Laughing, he nodded. "I'm working on it. Believe me."

Sighing, she imbibed the wine, trying to process the swirling emotions in her gut.

"Look, honey, if you don't want me to do it, I won't. But I can probably spin this into five hundred thousand extra a year for us."

"Five hundred thousand?" she asked, her eyes widening.

"Yep. Forget the four-bedroom house. I can buy you a ten-bedroom one."

"Not sure I need something that extravagant but Scott is working on a five-bedroom in the new development off Cyprus that I'm pretty enamored with."

"The extra bedroom would be helpful if we have a little girl," he said, winking.

Expelling a breath, she rubbed her hand over her face. "It's the embodiment of everything I fear. You leaving us to work in the city and realizing how much you miss it."

"Never going to happen," he said, resolute. "I'm exactly where I want to be."

Circling her wine glass on the table, she contemplated for so long, Peter waved his hand in front of her face. "Did I lose you?"

"Stop it," she playfully scolded, swatting his hand. "I'm thinking." Lifting the glass, she took the last sip. "You're not worried you're going to relapse? Or cheat on me?"

"Hell, no, on relapsing. If I never see another illicit drug in my life it will be too soon. And as far as cheating, I'm a lot of things but I'm not a cheater. I shouldn't have to tell you that."

"No, you were sure to break up with me before you were with anyone else."

"Are you trying to drag me into an argument?" he asked, hurt flashing across his features. "Because I'm not going there, Carrie. We've been doing so well and I have no desire to fight with you. If you're going to take digs, I'll just say 'no' off the bat. But you might want to think for one more moment what an opportunity like this can create for the kids."

"Sorry," she murmured, remorse setting in. "That was a low blow and you didn't deserve it. Pretty shitty of me to call you a cheater when I cheated on Jeff with you. He made a lot of mistakes but I hate that I cheated on him. It was only that one time but once is still too much."

"I mean, obviously, you couldn't control your ravenous desire for me."

"Um, right," she said, rolling her eyes. Tapping her nails on the table, she worked through the logistics. "How long will the entire process take before you don't have to trek into the city?"

"I think I can finalize the contracts by mid-November."

"Two months."

"Two months, tops," he said with a nod.

"And you really want to do this? It will make you happy?"

"You and the boys make me happy, hon, but it is exciting to use skills I haven't employed in so long. Not because I miss them, but because I have them and might as well use them to support our family."

"And I have your word you'll extricate yourself before the situation turns illegal or elicit, right?"

"You have my word. After all, who needs expensive call girls when I have Nurse Longwood? She's sexy as hell." He waggled his brows.

"Don't forget it, buddy."

Chuckling, he encircled her wrist and tugged her to sit on his lap. Sliding his fingers into the hair at the base of her scalp, he pulled her close, resting his forehead against hers. "I love you and I love the boys and I want to do this. You're going to have to trust me and I know that's really hard because I don't have the best track record. But I promise I won't let you down. Let me prove myself to you."

"You already have," she said, caressing his cheek. "You've made so many changes. I can tell how excited you are about this and I don't want to deny you."

"The opportunity is exciting, yes, but the ability to provide for us is my main motivation."

"Okay," she said, pressing a sweet kiss to his lips. "Go make us millionaires."

"Yeah?" he asked, elation in his blue eyes.

"Yeah. But sexy teacher is only coming out to play once your visits to the city are over. I bought the costume the other day. *That* should motivate you to complete the city portion of this venture as expeditiously as possible."

"Did I say five times? I meant I'd have to go into the city *zero* times. Yep, I'm done. Let's play."

Throwing back her head, she broke into joyful laughter. "Oh, no, buddy. I can offer shiny new things too. Can't wait to show you once the contract is secured."

Clutching her close, he drew her into a blazing kiss. Breathless, they panted, sharing the same breath as they gazed into each other's eyes.

"Thank you, honey," he said softly. "I'm excited to do this for us."

"I know. Thank you for putting us first. Please be patient with me because you know I'm going to worry about you every second you're in the city."

"I will. Open book, Carrie. I swear. You can call me anytime and I'll always answer or call you right back."

"Well, then, I think you have a phone call to make."

"Not for a while. Let's make out first."

Gliding her arms around his neck, her laughter surrounded them as he devoured her mouth with his.

The next evening, Peter sat at the long table inside the dim steakhouse, wondering when restaurants had become so loud. Everyone seemed to be conversing at the top of their lungs and he longed for the quiet of his hotel room.

"Stratford here knows everything about the Central Pennsylvania area and will run the hell out of the property," Bradley said, patting Peter on the back. "The man has limitless energy."

"Limitless is a bit of a stretch now that I'm nearing forty but I've still got some gas in the tank."

"Forty is young as hell, my friend," Larry Markinson, the investor, said across from him. "I'll be seventy-two next week and have never felt better. Of course, I thank the scotch and the firm for that. And I'll give Viagra a shout-out too," he said, lifting his glass.

"Cheers!" the men chimed, clanking glasses as Peter joined in with his iced tea.

"Well, I'm ready to make you a shit ton of money at the golf course, Mr. Markinson," he said. "Just tell me what I need to do get the contract finalized and let's get it done."

"Straight to the point. I like that, son. And call me Larry. For starters, I'd like to know if there's any way I can sway you drink a small sip of this fantastic scotch Bradley is buying me."

"Can't do it," Peter said, shaking his head as he smiled. "I could lie and tell you I miss it but I damn near disintegrated my liver when I used to drink and feel a hell of a lot better now."

"Well, at least you stand for something. I like that," he said, saluting before taking another sip.

"Plus, I donated a kidney to my kid and don't want to damage the one I have left."

"No shit?" Larry exclaimed, looking perplexed. "That's some serious dedication to family. Have to admire that, my boy."

"Thank you. I was happy to do it and my son is doing much better. It was an easy choice."

As the night wore on, Peter could see the admiration in Larry's eyes and developed a comradery with him that felt natural. Confident he would close the deal in record time, he murmured to Bradley, "How much of a cut is the firm getting for the referral?"

"We're taking ten percent of everything you earn, buddy," Bradley said softly. "You'll be making so much, you'll barely notice."

"Seven percent and we have a deal. I think I can close this guy during the next meeting."

Chuckling, he tilted his head. "I'll speak to the partners and see what I can do. Even though you're boring as hell, you're still a confident son of a bitch."

"What can I say?" Peter huffed on his nails and rubbed them on his shirt.

After dinner, the group headed to the hotel lobby for a nightcap, and Peter wished them goodnight. "It's almost midnight and I've got to call Carrie. Excited for our next meeting, Larry."

"Wish you'd stay and have one more, especially because I think Bradley might have secured other...entertainment, but I understand," Larry said, shaking his hand. "The pleasure is all mine and I look forward to working with you, Peter."

Once in the hotel room, Peter called Carrie as he lay atop the bed, hoping she wasn't pissed it was so late.

"Hey," her soft voice called over the phone.

"Hey, honey. We just finished. I'm sorry."

"I texted you but you didn't answer."

Feeling his brows draw together, he opened the text box and saw the unread texts. "Crap, I didn't even see them."

Silence crackled between them.

"I'll be home by three tomorrow, to answer you," he said, reading the texts. "I'm going to go into the office and negotiate some things with Bradley before I head home."

"Okay."

"I miss you."

"Miss you too."

The air was heavy between them and he longed to hold her. "We still splitting soccer duty tomorrow?"

"Yep. I'll take Charlie to his practice and you can go with Sebastian. Then, we'll switch for next week's practices."

"Got it. I enjoy watching them play. They're both getting really good."

"Sebastian says he wants to get a soccer scholarship. I'm here for it. Let's encourage him in case you can't close the deal."

"Shut your mouth, woman. I'm the best closer you've ever seen."

"Only took you thirty years with me, but, okay."

Chuckling, he picked at a string on the comforter. "You're my greatest conquest so it took a while longer."

"Man, you are good. That's a killer excuse."

"Can't wait to hold you tomorrow, honey. I'll call you when I'm close to Ardor Creek."

"Okay."

Peter thought about telling her he loved her but knew the stubborn woman most likely wouldn't say it back, especially with the strain of their current situation. Still, he'd learned many life lessons, and had observed Scott live with the regret of not saying the words one last time, so he forged ahead.

"I love you, Carrie."

Wispy breaths sounded in his ear. "Show me how much when you get home."

"Oh, that's definitely on the agenda. Dream of me tonight. I'll definitely be dreaming of sexy teacher."

Her chuckle traveled through the phone. "I have my ruler all ready for you, little boy."

"Okay, now I'm hard. Thanks a lot."

"Good night, Peter."

"Night, honey."

Clicking off the phone, he sank into the bed, missing her soft curves wrapped around him.

Chapter 22

♥

The next few weeks were frantic as Peter struggled to balance his trips into the city, his commitments at home, his local accounting clients, and managing Scott's books at GDC. He barely slept, sometimes choosing to drive home from the city late at night because it seemed to soothe Carrie, but there were times when staying over couldn't be avoided.

While he was in the city, Peter decided to also embark on a very important task: he was going to buy the perfect engagement ring for the woman he should've married ages ago. Since he'd royally screwed up so many times along the way, he was determined to use some of the new money he'd be earning to knock her socks off.

Marty Pomerantz, the owner of Pomerantz Fine Jewelry in New York City's Diamond District, had been one of Peter's favorite clients when he'd lived in the city. After finishing up a meeting with Larry, Bradley, and the rest of the partners one sunny mid-October afternoon, Peter whistled as he walked down the cobblestone sidewalk and entered the store.

"As I live and breathe," the gray-bearded man said from behind the counter as Peter approached. "The prodigal son returns. How the hell are you, Peter?"

"Pretty damn good, Marty," Peter said, shaking his hand. "How are you?"

"Eh, you know. I have too many grandkids to count which makes the wife happy. If the wife is happy, I can live another day."

Chuckling, Peter nodded. "Sound advice. Got anymore? I'm going to need it soon."

"No!" Marty said, silver eyes sparkling. "*You're* getting married? I remember you being wild as a hare before you left me with that Bradley Whitford. Nice guy but I still wonder if he's taking more commission than he deserves."

"Brad's honest," Peter said. "Aggressive but honest. You're in good hands. And, yes, I'm marrying the one who got away. I finally reeled her in again and I need to buy a ring that will make her reconsider when she wants to bolt."

"You, my friend, have come to the right place. Come over here and we'll start with this case," he said, waving Peter over to the glass display counter. "Anything you see can be personalized so be as detailed as you like. Let's get to work."

Two hours later, Peter's mind was spinning from the plethora of choices before him. Finally, he decided on a platinum ring with a square-cut diamond flanked by tiny emeralds that reminded him of Carrie's eyes. Hoping like hell she'd like it, Peter paid the down payment and Marty promised to have it sized and ready next week. The ring needed to be fashioned since it didn't originally come with the emeralds.

"Call me once you know the ring size and we'll be all set. I'm very happy for you, Peter."

"Fingers crossed she says 'yes,'" Peter said, shaking his hand.

Exiting the store, he called Ashlyn as he walked back to his car.

"Hey, Peter. How's it going?"

"Good. I have something I need to ask you and it has to remain top secret. I know that's almost impossible in Ardor Creek but I'm asking anyway."

"Sure, I'll try to help. Can I tell Scott?"

Peter contemplated. "He's pretty tight-lipped so, yeah, you can tell him but make sure he understands it has to stay between you two."

"Ohhhh, I like where this is going. Whatcha got?"

"How do I figure out what Carrie's ring size is?"

Silence answered him before Ashlyn emitted a huge "Woo hoo!" on the other end of the phone.

"Okay, Rivers, calm down," he teased, laughing. "It's time. Hell, it's been time for twenty years. I just ordered the ring and definitely need your help figuring out the size. I got her a really big diamond surrounded by a bunch of tiny emeralds because they're the color of her eyes. Is that cheesy?"

"Oh, Peter," she said, her tone laced with reverence. "It's absolutely perfect. She's going to die."

"Well, I hope not."

"You know what I mean. Okay, I'm on it. She and I are going shopping on Saturday. I'll find a way to work it into the conversation and report back. This is so exciting!"

"It really is. Thanks so much, Ashlyn. And remember, if you or Scott say anything, I'll have to kill you."

"My lips are sealed. Talk soon. Bye!"

Approaching his car which was parked along the sidewalk on one of the side streets, he slid behind the wheel and turned up the radio, hoping the catch the traffic report. By all accounts, there was a huge backup on the major thruway heading back to Pennsylvania. Glancing at the clock, he noticed it was almost four o'clock, which was the official start to rush hour in Manhattan. Hoping to beat the worst of it, he began the drive home.

Three hours later, Peter was still in Manhattan. Frustrated, he beat the wheel with his palm as he sat in the same spot on the West Side Highway he'd been sitting for thirty minutes. Annoyed and irritated, he called Carrie over Bluetooth.

"Hey, did the traffic let up?"

"I'm still in Manhattan," he said, craning his neck to see what was going on several car lengths ahead. "I tried to take the Lincoln Tunnel because the traffic reports said it was better but it was really congested so I hopped on the West Side Highway to take the George Washington Bridge. Now, it seems like there's an accident up ahead and the entire roadway is shut down. I haven't moved in half an hour."

"Yikes," she said, and Peter sensed her frustration. "I was really hoping to have you home for dinner tonight since you stayed in the city last night."

"I know, honey. I'm sorry."

"It's not your fault there's traffic. At least you're safe."

"I guess. I'm going to try to get off the next exit and see if the Lincoln Tunnel has cleared up. I'll do my best to get home tonight."

"As opposed to *not* coming home?"

"At this rate, I could end up sitting on the highway for hours. If that happens, I'll probably just grab a hotel room and head home in the morning."

"I see."

"You sound pissed, Carrie. I understand but it's not fair to blame me for something I can't control."

"Tonight will make six."

"Six what?"

"If you stay over tonight, it will be six nights you've stayed in the city to close this deal. Six nights I've had to manage the boys' schedules without you and explain to them why you're not home. This is what I was afraid of, Peter."

Inhaling a deep breath, he told himself to remain calm although irritation burned in his gut.

"Seriously, Carrie?"

"What? Do you not want me to be honest? I did fine on my own as a single parent and I can do it again. I'd started depending on you but I guess that's too much to ask since this project dropped in your lap."

"That's so incredibly unfair, I'm not going to honor it with a response. I'm doing this for you and the boys, and that's all."

"The boys whose soccer games you missed last week because Bradley needed you at the fancy Italian restaurant in Midtown?"

Slapping the wheel with his hand, Peter felt his control begin to slip. "Fuck this. I'm not doing this on the phone with you, Carrie."

"Fine! Stay in the city tonight. I don't want you here anyway."

"For god's sake—"

"I mean it, Peter. I have to go. I'm cooking yet another dinner where I'll explain to the boys why you're not here. Making excuses for you is getting really old. Maybe you can have dinner with Bradley since you don't have time for us. Goodbye."

The phone clicked off and music flooded the car in its wake. Rubbing his eyes with his thumb and index finger, Peter groaned.

Annoyed at the entire situation, he pulled up the traffic app on his phone and attempted to find a faster way home...if he ever moved from the damn spot in which he was currently stuck.

An hour and a half later, the accident ahead was removed and traffic began to slowly move but only scant inches at a time. By ten o'clock, Peter hadn't even made it to the George Washington Bridge yet. Even if he crossed the bridge, the drive to Ardor Creek would take two and a half hours. Feeling exhaustion creep in, he pulled off the slow-moving highway and used his travel app to find a hotel.

Once he was settled in, he texted Carrie as he lay in bed.

Peter: I'm really sorry, Care Bear. I'll make it up to you. You have to know I'd rather be holding you now than sleeping in this shitty hotel.

The text bubble appeared and he could all but see her furiously typing in their bedroom as smoke threatened to puff from her ears.

Carrie: It is what it is. I'll see you when you get to the office tomorrow. Night.

Man, she was pissed. He could tell by the shortness of her text. Vowing to make it up to her tomorrow, he relaxed into the bed, noting the soreness from sitting in the car for so long. Willing his muscles to ease the tension, he tried to get some sleep.

Chapter 23

October barreled into November as Peter solidified the contracts with Larry's attorneys. His friend and local attorney, Mark Lancaster, represented him in the transaction and he was relieved to be in the home stretch. Carrie's resentment of his time spent in the city had grown and he couldn't wait to be home on a full-time basis so he could focus on the family.

Sebastian and Charlie's soccer leagues were winding down and would end right before Thanksgiving. It meant they all would get a reprieve from their breakneck schedules, and Peter looked forward to family nights at home, eating dinner together and watching movies. Chuckling to himself as he manned the grill on the back porch one evening, he smiled as Carrie's arms surrounded him from behind.

"What are you laughing at over here?" she asked, resting her cheek on his back.

"Just thinking how awesome it will be to chill at home with you and the boys without having anything on the schedule."

"Sounds amazing," she said wistfully.

"Yep." He flipped over the burgers, happy to offer her a night off from cooking. "It's just funny because if you'd asked me ten years ago, or even five years ago, a night like that would've seemed like torture. Now, it's all I want."

"We've both been burning the candle at both ends. The holidays will be a nice break. Ashlyn called today and wants to have a big Thanksgiving meal at her house since the baby's due any day. That way, they won't have to travel and I can help her cook. You in?"

"Yep," he said, pressing a burger with the spatula. "Scott told me about it today and it sounds perfect. I think they invited half the town."

"Works for me. I can help cook and clean up but I don't have to host or clean this wreck of a house. I'm thrilled."

"Sounds like a plan. What time do they want us over there on Thanksgiving Day?"

"She said any time after two is fine. I'll pick out something for the boys to wear besides the normal ratty t-shirts and frayed sneakers."

"Chad will be there right?" he asked, referring to the mayor.

"Yep. He's still dating Britney but told me last week he doesn't like the way she chews. He has a gift for finding flaws in every woman he dates and eventually sending them on their way."

"I'm betting someone will come along and knock his socks off. He's kind of a man-whore so he needs a woman who won't take his shit."

"I'll believe it when I see it, but your turnaround gives me hope," she teased, squeezing him.

Peter's mind churned as a plan formulated. The engagement ring was now in his possession—hidden in the tackle box in the basement so Carrie wouldn't find it—and he was ready to propose. Thanks to Ashlyn's sleuthing skills, he'd reported Carrie's ring size to Marty and thought the ring exceptional. Hoping Carrie would feel the same, he pondered the pieces of his plan.

"You got quiet there, mister," she said, peeking over his shoulder. "I think the burgers are done."

"Yep. Let me load them up and I'll bring them inside," he said, placing a kiss on her forehead.

As she set the table and rounded up the boys for dinner, Peter's body hummed with the anticipation of finally asking the love of his life to marry him. Trepidation laced his veins as he realized there was still a small kernel of fear deep in his gut she might say 'no'. The last few weeks had been difficult and their relationship was strained by his new project. And, much to his dismay, she still hadn't looked him deep in the eyes and uttered the words he was dying to hear.

Wondering why, he sighed as he loaded up the burgers. Kara would be watching the boys on Friday so they could go to dinner at the pub, and he was determined to get to the bottom of her reluctance once and for all.

Letting the worry go for the moment, he headed inside to have dinner.

U nfortunately, Friday's date never happened. Peter headed into the city on Friday morning, elated it would be the last time. The final contracts were ready to be signed and, moving forward, everything could be handled from Peter's Ardor Creek office. Or, so he thought.

When Peter entered the board room at Bradley's firm, he noticed a vacancy at the long mahogany table.

"Where's Larry?"

"We've had quite a fortuitous turn of events, buddy," Bradley said, approaching and patting him on the back. "Larry is working from his home in Napa this weekend and wants us to fly there to finalize everything. His private plane is gassed up and waiting for us at Teterboro Airport."

"Are you insane?" Peter asked, hands extended at his side. "I have a family who's expecting me home in a few hours. I can't fly to Napa."

"Bring the wife with you. Larry said she was welcome although I don't think he's open to the kids coming along."

"Holy shit," Peter said, resting his forehead on his palm. "What a fucking dick move. There's no way I'm getting on a plane to sign the paperwork. We can do it remotely while I'm here."

"He was clear that you sign in Napa or you don't sign at all. Larry's taken a liking to you and I think he has an ulterior motive. He's also building a golf course in Northern California and wants to show you the property. I think he wants you to manage that one too."

"No fucking way. I'm not interested in managing anything that requires me to travel."

"Wow, the redhead really has you on a leash. Are you really going to turn down an opportunity like that?"

"Yes, I really am." Huffing a frustrated breath, Peter slumped into one of the chairs, feeling defeated.

"Look, whether you're interested in the new property or not, Larry's adamant he won't sign the deal anywhere but Napa. Are you going to throw everything you've accomplished over the past two months down the drain? Not to mention, you'll be opening yourself up for a ton of expense and possible litigation if it falls through."

"You guys would really be that petty?"

"Look, man, this firm cares about one thing, and it's money. I don't have to tell you that. If the Scranton deal with Larry falls through, the firm will back bill you for all the dinners and hours spent on your meetings. They were happy to foot the bill when they knew they were getting seven percent of your future earnings but if that disappears, they'll invoice you for every single penny. Plus, Larry is a litigious son of a bitch. If I were you, I'd just go to Napa for the weekend and close the damn deal."

"The weekend?" Peter asked, exasperated.

"Larry's set on showing you the course tomorrow and signing the paperwork on Sunday morning. You'd be home by Sunday evening and everything would be finalized."

Expelling a breath through puffed cheeks, Peter shook his head. "I can't man. This will destroy my relationship. I just can't do it."

"If you can't, you can't," Bradley said, shrugging. "You'd be gaining a ton of problems to save one weekend but it's up to you. I'll give you a few minutes to think about it before we head to the airport."

Left alone in the room, Peter contemplated the terrible choice before him. Although he'd love to whisk Carrie away for a weekend in Napa, there was no way she could leave on such short notice. The boys had games and piano this weekend, among other things. Furious at the situation, he bit the bullet and called her.

"Hey. How did the contract signing go? Are you finished already?"

"It didn't go," he said, not even masking his irritation. Updating her on the situation, he listened to her strained silence on the other end.

"If I don't go and get it done, they're going to back bill me for everything, Carrie. It will cost me hundreds of thousands of dollars once I cover the firm's legal fees. I don't see how I can get out of it."

Quiet crackles sounded along with her breathing.

"I'm so sorry, honey. I wish I could find another solution. I don't want to throw away all this hard work when we're so close."

"So, you're just going to hop on a plane and go to California?"

"A guy like Larry will have a guest house with everything I need. I wouldn't have time to drive back to Ardor Creek before the plane departs."

"I see."

"If you don't want me to go, I won't. It's an impossible situation."

"Actually, it doesn't seem that impossible to me. It's the embodiment of everything I feared when you decided to pursue this venture. First, it's an extra night away in the city. Then, it's a trip to Napa. Then, it's multiple projects where you're flying all over the country and never home. One day, we'll wake up and realize we never see each other and have become strangers."

"Wow, that's a pretty big leap, Carrie. I'm not interested in managing the Napa project and will make that clear."

"But if you capitulate now, you give him the power to do this again. Don't you see, Peter? And if I capitulate, I'm doing the same thing. I learned that lesson with you so many times and I refuse to repeat it. You can go to Napa but don't expect to return home to us. I'm not doing this with you again."

"Whoa, wait. What? You can't be serious, Carrie—"

"I've never been more serious in my life, Peter. I told you, it would be different if it were only me, but I'm not doing this to our boys. Go to Napa. I understand why you need to do it. You've gotten yourself into a terrible situation. But when you come home, you need to move back into your house."

"I'm about to accept an offer on the house. We discussed this two days ago."

"I don't think you should accept it. We need to take a step back and reevaluate. We moved too fast. I'll take responsibility for that. I was so grateful for what you did for Sebastian and how hard you tried in the beginning—"

"I'm trying now!" he screamed, tamping down the urge to shatter the phone against the wall. "Don't you get that? I'm doing this for us."

"So you keep saying but what's the point in having more money if you're beholden to this investor. He seems like an ass and is really disrespectful of your time."

Digesting her words, he admitted she was right. If he did go to Napa, he needed to have a detailed conversation with Larry about boundaries. That was for damn sure.

"Go, Peter. I don't want to fight with you. Do what you need to do and close the deal. I'll box your stuff up and have it ready for you to pick up when you get home."

Peter felt the sting of tears as he buried his head in his hand. "Carrie..."

"Go, Peter. I'm done with this conversation. We'll see you on Sunday."

Exhaling a breath, he said, "I'll call you when I land."

"Don't bother. I'll be busy with the boys. We'll talk on Sunday. Be safe. Goodbye."

The phone went dead in his hand, mimicking the deadened heart that now sat shattered inside his chest. Furious at the world, he stood and prepared to head to California.

By the time Peter arrived in Napa on Friday afternoon, he was ready to give Larry a piece of his mind. When he, Bradley, and the two other partners who'd accompanied them entered the expansive estate, they found Larry on the back porch drinking scotch. He rose and seemed quite jovial as he noticed Peter's expression.

"Why so sad, my boy?" he asked, extending his hand for a shake. "Is it really a hardship to have a weekend away in Napa?"

"When I have to leave my family behind, yes, it is," Peter said, reluctantly shaking his hand. "I need to make one thing clear, Larry. I won't put this project in front of my family. If you're not okay with that, you need to find someone else. I'm only here because I'm loath to throw away weeks of hard work and negotiation."

"I understand," Larry said, patting his shoulder. "Laura, get this man an iced tea," he called to the housekeeper. "Or do you want something stronger?"

"Tea is fine. Thank you. I'd like to discuss the schedule for the weekend."

"Bradley already informed me you're not interested in managing the Napa golf course but I'd like an opportunity to change your mind. We'll visit it tomorrow and sign the paperwork for the Scranton course on Sunday."

"I won't change my mind but you seem dead set on trying so I'll accompany you tomorrow as a show of good faith."

"Excellent," Larry said, urging him to sit. "For now, let's enjoy this magnificent November California weather." Resigning himself to the circumstances, Peter settled in for a long night of scotch he couldn't drink and conversation in which he had to participate, whether he liked it or not.

Chapter 24

♥

Carrie awoke Saturday her normal chipper self...which meant she wanted to strangle any living being who came within fifty feet. Unfortunately, her son appeared at her bedside, and being that she loved him dearly, she decided to let him live.

"Morning, buddy. What's up?"

"Charlie came inside my fort again, Mom!" Sebastian said, holding up one of his action figures. "See? He broke off the arm. He has to buy me another one out of his allowance!"

"I didn't do it!" Charlie yelled, running into the room. "You broke it and you want a new one so you're blaming it on me."

"Did not!"

"Did too!"

"Okay, okay," Carrie said, sitting up and holding up her palms. "Enough! I'm not starting this morning with you two screaming at each other. I was going to cook omelets but if you don't stop arguing, we'll have Raisin Bran instead."

"No, Mom! I hate Raisin Bran," Sebastian whined.

"Then stop fighting with your brother right now." Charlie stuck out his tongue at Sebastian. "And if I see that tongue one more time today, young man, you're not playing soccer. Got it?"

Charlie nodded as tears welled in his eyes, sending a huge spear of pain through her heart. "Let me get dressed and I'll be right down. Can you set the table for me?"

They both uttered in agreement before bolting from the room. Lying back on the bed, she groaned and rubbed her eyes. Sprawling her arm over the pillow beside her, she clutched it, feeling her own tears well at how much she missed Peter. She longed for him so vehemently, she closed her eyes and wished for one moment to be blessed with the power of transportation. She'd zoom to California and whisk him away so he could come home and fill the void created by his absence.

But this was real life so Carrie dragged herself out of bed, threw on sweats, and made breakfast for the boys. Charlie had a soccer game at noon and Peter had planned on taking Sebastian hiking but those plans had disintegrated when he flew across the country. Feeling the anger bubble inside her gut, she clenched her teeth as she got ready to transport her heathens all over town.

Once they made it to the field, she settled in for a long day of listening to fellow moms chatter on about a million things. She half-listened to conversations about the upcoming bake sale, the Thanksgiving parade, and other happenings around town. Charlie did quite well in his game and ran over to her after making a goal in the second half.

"Did you see, Mom? I kicked it right past his head."

"I saw," she said, hugging him as she crouched down. "Great job, buddy."

"Can we call Uncle Peter tonight and tell him?"

"Peter's away for work, honey, but he'll be back on Monday and we'll tell him all about it, okay?"

Brown hair swished as he furiously nodded before rejoining the game. Glancing over, Carrie noticed Sebastian sitting in the grass with Selina, one of his friends who played in his soccer league. They seemed to be examining a nearby anthill and having a grand ol' time. Every so often, Sebastian would pick up one of the tiny critters and show it to her before dropping it back to the ground and devolving into laughter. Selina playfully slapped his shoulder each time before her son's cheeks blazed red.

Gazing on the revelry, she realized something profound: her son had a crush. It was so achingly sweet to watch him interact with Selina and reminded her so much of her exchanges with Peter at that age. Allowing the yearning to set in, her thoughts drifted to all those small moments that comprised their storied history. Peter was so embedded in her life, she had no idea how to extricate him from it. And, if she was honest with herself, she had no desire to.

Once the exhausting day was over and the boys were finally asleep, Carrie lay in the lonely bed, soaking up the quiet as the ceiling fan whooshed above. Inhaling deep breaths, she embraced her anger, evaluating its origins. After some intense reflection, she realized she wasn't really mad at Peter. Sure, she was angry and that was justified to an extent, but she knew his intentions were pure. Instead, what she actually felt in her core was fear. It was heavy and uncomfortable, representing all her pent-up resentment from his past desertions.

Recognizing the terror for what it was, Carrie contemplated whether she truly wanted to take a break. She'd indicated as much to Peter when she told him to move back home, but that had stemmed from anger. In reality, she'd come to rely on him, as her partner...her lover...and, most significantly, her best friend. Yes, somewhere along the way, he'd become her rock. It was the place he'd occupied in her heart so very long ago and, in that profound moment, she understood it was the most important.

"I'm not alone anymore," she said softly, the words strange upon her lips. "You don't have to do this alone, Carrie."

The fan whirled above, dispersing the words throughout the room. Accepting them was foreign but she let them into her petrified heart anyway. For a woman who'd fought every damn battle of her life alone, she finally had a bunker mate. And she knew without a doubt, Peter would jump in front and take a hundred bullets to prevent even one from grazing her.

Needing to process the realization, she didn't answer Peter's text when her phone lit up on the nightstand, as she hadn't answered the others he'd sent. After all, what they needed to discuss couldn't be done over text and she truly wanted him to focus on closing this deal so he could hurry the hell home. And, even though she'd experienced a pretty intense realization, she was still pissed. Oh, yeah, he was still in deep shit. She'd make him pay her in bubble baths where she read sexy books on her tablet and drank wine while he cooked dinner for the boys...for a week. No, for *several* weeks. Smiling at the decadent image, Carrie clicked off the light and pulled the pillow close, although it was a poor substitute for Peter's strong arms.

On Saturday, Larry showed Peter the site of the new golf course, which was impressive.

"You'll do well with this site," Peter said. "It's within driving distance of several wineries and the land is laid out perfectly. I can see why you chose it."

"I want you to manage it, Peter. I'm firm in that decision."

"I have no desire to do it and you'd be better served by someone who's completely dedicated. I'm sorry, Larry. It's better if we're honest with each other."

"We'll see," he said, taking a puff of his cigar. "I think I can win you over if I throw enough money your way."

"Not this time," Peter said, admiring his persistence. "But I'm flattered."

That evening, Peter slogged through an expensive dinner at one of the best restaurants in Napa. Sitting at the table surrounded by his old partners, he questioned what the hell he was doing. He should be at home with Carrie and the boys, grilling hot dogs and playing the new video game with them. Years ago, he would've loved being wined and dined at a fancy restaurant by a rich investor. Now, he was just lonely and miserable, and missed his family.

He'd tried to call Carrie several times, but it always went to voicemail and his texts went unanswered. Realizing what a mess he'd made, he couldn't wait to fly home and fix it. Carrie was pissed as hell but he wouldn't go down without a fight. They'd come too far this time and he was determined to forge ahead and repair their relationship.

On Sunday morning, he sat with Larry and the team at the estate's large dining table. A speakerphone sat in the middle so attorneys for both parties could listen. Dragging the contracts across the table, Larry rested his palm over the stack of papers.

"Everything is here and ready to be signed," Larry said. "I've also prepared documents for the Napa golf course as well. I hate to play hardball this late in the game, Peter, but if you won't consider managing the Napa course, I refuse to sign the papers for Scranton."

Peter saw red as his gaze swung to Bradley, who shrugged as if to say, *Well, what are you going to do now?*

"Thank you for the offer, Larry. It's truly appreciated but I'm only interested in managing and advising the financials at the Scranton location. You brought me here to sign the contract and I've been extremely understanding. Slide them over and let's seal this deal. I'm ready to make you a ton of money in Scranton and will happily work remotely with anyone you hire to manage Napa."

"It's not going to happen, son," Larry said, sitting back in his chair. "All or nothing. I'm sorry to put you in this position but I know a good investment when I see it and I want it all."

Sighing, Peter stood and ran a hand through his hair. Gaining the courage to do what he should've done weeks ago, he shook his head. "I wish you the best of luck, then. If my attorney contacts you regarding breach of contract, know it isn't personal, Larry. I'm sorry we couldn't make this work." Giving a nod, he pivoted and began to walk away.

"Peter!" Larry called, standing and gesturing with his hand. "You can't be serious! This is a fantastic opportunity. You're going to throw everything down the drain now?"

Turning, Peter lifted his chin, defiant. "I've been focusing on the wrong thing my entire life and almost fell into that trap again. I appreciate you reminding me why I left this world in the first place. Now, if you'll excuse me, I've got to go apologize to my family for not putting them first for several weeks now. And you should really think about your business practices, Larry. They're underhanded and pretty fucking dishonest. Good luck with the courses." After one last glare for good measure, Peter trailed through the hallway and out the front door.

Pulling up his phone, he secured a rideshare and waited a few minutes before it drove up and transported him to the airport. After securing a standby flight home, Peter texted Carrie.

Peter: I know you hate me right now but I just told Larry to fuck off. It's going to cost me a shit ton of money but I'm done with his bullshit. You were right about everything, Carrie. I'm so sorry. I miss you and the boys so much. I'll be home around seven p.m. Can we talk tonight?

The boarding announcement boomed overhead and he hoped she'd text him back before he departed. After a minute, the bubble appeared and he swallowed the dread in the back of his throat.

Carrie: Kara can watch the kids while we talk. I'll meet you at your house at seven.

The words were succinct, shooting a spark of fear down his spine.

Peter: Don't give up on us. Please, Carrie. See you at seven. I'll text you if anything changes. I can't wait to hug you.

Carrie: See you at seven. Be safe.

Sighing, Peter scrubbed his hand over his face and waited to board.

Hours later, Peter entered his darkened house, hating that it had come to represent everything he detested. His old life. His former self. All the mistakes he'd made. Most things had been boxed and were ready to donate to charity or had already been moved to Carrie's house. The couch still sat in the living room, although all the other furniture was gone, and he sat on it, dejected, as he waited for her.

When she hadn't appeared by eight o'clock, Peter wondered if she was going to stand him up. He shot her a text to which she gave a short reply that she was running late and would be over soon. Feeling restless in the silent house, he rummaged through some of the boxes in the kitchen until he found what he was looking for. Sliding down the wall, he sat on the cold floor and waited for her to appear...

Chapter 25

Carrie entered the dim foyer of Peter's home, noticing the light shining from the kitchen. Trailing down the hallway, she found him sitting on the kitchen floor, back against the wall as he held something in his hand.

"Hey," she said, lowering to sit beside him. "What you got there?"

"A tumbler," he said, lifting it so she could see the glass. "Unwrapped it from the boxes I packed for charity over there." He gestured toward the boxes across the room.

"Okay," she said, eyebrows drawing together. "Do you want me to put some water in it?"

He shook his head, his expression forlorn. "After rehab, I'd hold one of these and test the weight in my hand, remembering how good it felt to drink. Drinking always numbed the self-loathing and made the problems go away for a while."

Compassion filtered through her at his pain. Although she was angry, she'd always hated seeing Peter suffer. Aching to soothe him, she cupped his shoulder. "I'm sorry you're hurting, Peter. I really am."

The corner of his lips curved as he stared into her eyes. "This is pretty much how it happened," he said softly.

"How what happened?"

"How I fell in love with you. You looked at me exactly like you are now and soothed me after that jerk threw a dodgeball at my face."

Carrie breathed a laugh. "Well, that's a full-circle moment right there if I've ever seen one."

Laughing, he nodded. "It definitely is."

Sliding her fingers over the tumbler, she asked, "Can I set this on the counter? You don't need it, Peter. We're going to be okay. I know we are."

Releasing the glass, he nodded. Carrie stood and placed it on the island before sitting back down.

"How do you know?" he asked.

"Because I realized something while you were away," she said, turning to face him. "We're the best versions of ourselves when we're together. Conversely, we're pretty shitty when we're apart. So, we're going to figure out a way to be together and we're going to make it work."

He slid his hand over her jean-clad thigh, giving her that adorable smile. "I'm definitely a mess without you, Carrie. I don't know what the hell I was thinking. I honestly entered into the situation with Larry with good intentions."

"I know you did. I thought about it a lot over the past few days. I think I wanted it to fail."

He lifted an eyebrow. "You *think*?"

Chuckling, she covered his hand atop her thigh. "I was so afraid to go all-in with you even though you were pushing full steam ahead and doing everything right. You were extremely patient with me and I still held back."

"Yeah, that really sucked. It broke my heart you wouldn't say you loved me, honey. I don't get it because I know you do."

"At least his ego is intact," she muttered.

"Come on," he said, grinning as he squeezed her leg. "You've loved me ever since you saw my neck swollen like a damn watermelon. That's really sexy. You had no choice."

Rolling her eyes, she slid her leg over his thighs and straddled him, shimmying over his lap. Cupping his face, she stared into the blue irises she'd memorized years ago. "Even though you're teasing me, it's absolutely true. I love you, Peter, and have for as long as I can remember. Which is why it hurt so badly each time you left. I was so afraid to say it to you this time because I knew if we screwed it up, we probably wouldn't get another shot. And, then, you got that stupid call from Bradley."

"I should've hung up on him," Peter joked, threading his fingers through the hair at her temple. "Should've just stayed focused on my clients in Ardor Creek. I'm so sorry, honey."

"No, I'm sorry," she said, shaking her head. "The second you told me about the opportunity, it all came crashing down. All my hopes this time would be different. I didn't even give it a chance. By the time you called me to tell me you were flying to Napa, I pretty much wanted to chop you up into little pieces and bury them all over Pennsylvania."

"Yikes. Am I safe in the house alone with you? That's some serial killer stuff right there."

"It's true. I was pretty much plotting your demise. But then, I was at Charlie's soccer game yesterday and he made a goal and ran over to hug me. He smiled up at me with that adorable gap from the tooth you helped him pull and told me how excited he was to tell you about it when you got home."

Emotion swam in Peter's eyes as she spoke the reverent words.

"And Sebastian has his first crush. I noticed it when they were playing on the sidelines at Charlie's game. When I asked him if he wanted to tell me anything about Selina, he brushed it off. But, last night, he kept asking me questions about when you were coming home. My mother's intuition tells me he'd rather talk to *you* about Selina, which is really cute."

"I can tell him how I talked you into kissing me with tongue when we were in fifth grade."

"You will do no such thing, Peter Stratford," she scolded, swatting his shoulder. "You'll tell him to be a good, respectful boy and wait to ask her out until she's at least sixteen."

"Uh, okay. Yeah, sure. That's what I'll say."

Laughing, she bit her lip as she studied him. "They both got sick tonight, which is why I was late. The cake from the birthday party earlier today made all the kids sick. There's a furious mom text chain going around that I can't wait to show you. Anyway, while they were puking their guts out, I just kept thinking how badly I wanted you there with me."

"Sounds pretty gross but I'm glad I'm approved for puke duty."

"Oh, you're always approved for that, buster."

"Oh, joy. Go on. You were pouring your heart out to me. Keep it up." He slid his hands over her waist and cupped the mounds of her butt, pulling her in closer.

"What I was saying," she said, exasperated, "is that somewhere along the way, I began to rely on you and, even though I can do this without you, I realized I don't want to. Loving you was never the issue. Being vulnerable enough to trust you was always my biggest reservation. But I'm finally there, Peter. Just like you finally made it to the point where you're ready to commit. I'm finally ready to let you into every piece of my heart."

"Does that mean you'll stop threatening to kick me out every time I fuck up? Because that's some Defcon One level stuff, Carrie. You're going to have to let me make mistakes. I'm new at this whole dad, partner, overall-awesome-human-being thing."

"You're not terrible at it," she said, wrinkling her nose.

"Thanks for the vote of confidence."

"And it doesn't hurt that you're so sexy," she whispered before trailing her thumb over his lips.

He exhaled a ragged breath, heavy with desire. "Carrie..."

"Letting you in means you're going to hurt me sometimes," she continued, giving a resigned shrug. "I was so terrified of that until I finally accepted that love is messy. It's awful and amazing and strange and overpowering all at once. When you came home so excited about the new venture, it hurt, because it made me feel like we weren't enough for you."

"I'm sorry," he whispered. "That wasn't how I felt, Carrie. I swear."

"I know. Those were my old fears manifesting in this new version of our relationship and that wasn't fair. If we're going to do this, I have to be strong enough to let those old fears go. Your sobriety is really inspiring to me. The way you released all those demons and doubts...well, if you can do it, I can let go of my fears too."

"We'll do it together," he said, pulling her close and nuzzling her nose with his. "We've done so much better this time around. A few shitty weeks doesn't negate that fact."

"Nope," she said, giving him a soft kiss. "I'm determined to figure it out, Peter. I love you too much to fail."

"I love you so much, Care Bear," he murmured before capturing his lips with hers. Their tongues battled as she squirmed atop his lap, so happy to be in his arms once again.

"Thank god you finally said you love me back because I'm screwed, by the way. The firm is going to take me to the cleaners and a billionaire investor is probably going to sue me. I'm a real catch over here."

"You never understood I didn't give a crap about your accolades or money, Peter. All I ever wanted was you."

"Well, that's great, because I might be a bum tomorrow morning. Please take me in. I'll give up every major organ for shelter."

Laughing, she pulled him close. "One kidney was enough. I'll shelter you forever for that gift. You're amazing, Peter. I'm sorry I was so hard on you. I promise I'm going to do better."

"Me too, honey," he said against her lips. "We're going to get it right this time. It might not be perfect, but it's going to be right and that's all we need."

After thoroughly kissing her again, he asked, "Can I come home now? I miss the boys and want to see them, even if they're sleeping."

"Yes," she said, sliding off his lap and extending her hand. "Come on. Let's go home."

Grasping tightly, she led him away from his past and into their future together.

Chapter 26

Peter charged into Monday morning, ready to take the offensive against the onslaught of litigation that was sure to come. Sitting in his office at GDC, he spoke to Mark Lancaster on the phone as he squinted at the monitor.

"There's definitely some language regarding 'good faith' in the contract," Peter said, scrolling through the document. "I think we can make a case that Larry negotiated in bad faith and prove he didn't disclose his true intentions regarding the Napa project."

"I can definitely make that case," Mark said, relaying confidence that reassured Peter. "Let me get to work on some preliminary arguments so they'll be ready when we receive the paperwork from Larry's attorneys."

"Thanks, man. I should've known when you decimated everyone on the debate team junior year those skills would come in handy one day. Never understood why you stayed in Ardor Creek and didn't move to L.A. or New York to become District Attorney."

"I like practicing law in Lackawanna County and have actually been mulling a run here."

"Lackawanna County D.A.?"

"Yep. You were the best gambler I knew before you gave it up. What do you think my odds are?"

"Pretty damn good. You're young, good looking and a hell of an attorney. Wow, Mark, that's great."

"We'll see," he said, slightly hesitant. "Mom told me I need to get married because single candidates don't poll well with middle-aged men."

"Probably because the middle-aged housewives will fantasize about you while their husbands are playing golf."

His deep chuckle reverberated through the phone. "Maybe. Glad you've still got your sense of humor, Peter. Don't get down about the situation. Litigation could take months and maybe even years and most wealthy people get bored after the initial anger dies down. And if the firm back bills you, I can make a case against them for so many SEC violations, their heads will spin. Purchasing high-end escorts for a client has not, and never will be, legal. We'll fry those bastards."

"Thanks, buddy. I'm so glad you're in my corner here. As far as the other matter we discussed, you'll be able to guide us through the license process if all goes according to plan?"

"Yep. Chad will do his part and I'll be happy to help solidify everything for you guys afterward. This is going to be the most epic Thanksgiving meal I've ever attended."

"We'll see. I'm still on thin ice but Carrie's been pretty cool even though I might have dragged her into the poor house with me."

"Did I hear my name?" Carrie asked, entering the office and setting a brown bag on the desk. "Ashlyn made beef empanadas today," she said, giving a dramatic chef's kiss. "They're amazing. Had to bring you some."

"I'm going to hop off, Mark. Call me with any updates. Thanks."

Hanging up the phone, he grinned as he peeked in the bag. "These smell fantastic."

"They're so good," she said, lowering into the chair in front of his desk. "I might have eaten two...and then gone back and bought two more. Will you still love me if I have extra empanada dimples on my thighs?"

Laughing, he nodded. "As long as you still love me when I'm broke and destitute."

"I know you'll figure it out," she said, sitting up and squeezing his wrist. "Dig in and then update me on your conversation with Mark."

He updated her before she returned to her desk and waited for Scott to return from a site visit. When his friend arrived, Peter strolled into his office and shut the door before sitting down.

"What's up, man?" Scott asked.

"I have a favor to ask you and it's short notice but I think you'll do it for me."

"Okay, I can certainly try. What is it?"

Smiling, Peter relaxed in the chair and laced his fingers behind his head. "This might be a strange question but have you ever built an altar?"

Scott's eyebrows drew together. "I've built everything at this point. Who needs an altar?"

Peter's grin deepened and Scott beamed.

"Oh, man, this is going to be good."

"Buckle up, buddy, and let me tell you what I've got in mind..."

Pulsing with excitement, Peter explained his master plan.

Peter watched the boys on Saturday so Carrie could go visit Ashlyn, who'd just brought baby Grant home. She was so excited about the new addition to Scott and Ashlyn's family which spurred hope she was still on board with having another baby. In the meantime, Peter had something extremely important to discuss with the two kids they already had. He'd informed Carrie last night that he wanted to ask the boys to call him Dad instead of Uncle Peter if they felt comfortable. She'd given him a huge smile and urged him to discuss it with them while she was visiting Ashlyn.

"Hey, guys," Peter said, crawling through the opening in the large bush Charlie used for his fort. It was a massive holly bush with thick branches that sat at the edge of Carrie's property. The inside was hollow, making it a perfect place to hide if you were an eight-year-old boy.

"Hey, Uncle Peter," Charlie said. "We're playing Hulk versus Black Widow. Want to play?"

"Sure do. I'll take Thor but I want to talk to you guys first," he said, wiping dirt off his jeans and facing them as he sat cross-legged in the cramped space.

"Okay," they said in unison.

"First of all, I love it when you guys call me Uncle Peter, but now that I live with you guys, I was hoping you might want to call me Dad. What do you think about that?"

They stared at him, wide-eyed, as they contemplated.

"You're my real dad, anyway, so I don't mind," Sebastian said, shrugging. "I kind of think of you as my dad already since you take me to practice and hang out with us all the time."

Peter smiled. "It makes me really happy to hear that, Sebastian. What about you, Charlie?"

"I wish you were my real dad," he said softly.

"I am, buddy," he said, scooting over and pulling the tyke on his lap. "In every way that matters. Right here," he said, covering his chest with his palm.

Charlie also covered his heart and gazed up at him with those wide brown eyes. They were so open and deep—so much like Carrie's—that Peter felt a jolt in his solar plexus.

"Yep, right in your heart," Peter said, kissing the boy's thick hair. "I love you guys. You know that, right?"

"We know," Sebastian said, the dimple showing as he smiled.

"We love you too," Charlie said.

Peter welled up like a damn heartbroken teenager watching a rom-com. "Come here," he whispered, pulling Sebastian close and embracing them in a huge bear hug. After one last firm squeeze, he released them and settled back in for the next big discussion.

"Okay, now that we've established my 'Dad status,'" he teased, making quotation marks with his fingers, "I need to speak to you guys about something very important that's extremely top secret."

Their spines straightened as they nodded, rapt with attention.

"I mean it, guys," he said, holding up his finger, "super-top secret. It can't go beyond this fort and we definitely can't tell your mom."

"Mom says we shouldn't lie," Charlie said.

"She's absolutely right about that," he said, tilting his head, "but you *can* keep secrets in very special circumstances when you know it will make someone really happy. And I'm hoping this secret will make your mom happy."

"You want to marry her!" Sebastian exclaimed.

Chuckling, he ruffled his hair. "Yep, I want to marry her. And I need your help to make it perfect. But before that, I need your permission. You're the two most important people in her life and I don't want to marry her if either of you doesn't want me to."

"Why wouldn't we want you to?" Charlie asked.

"I don't know," he said, shrugging. "But it's important you tell me if you have any concerns or questions about us getting married. I want to be a part of your family in every way but only if you want me to be."

"I want you to be our family!" Charlie said.

"Me too," Sebastian chimed.

"Whew," he said, dramatically swiping his forehead with his arm. "Thank goodness. I was worried you guys would grill me."

They both snickered as he contorted his features into a goofy expression.

"Being part of your family means I'm going to adopt you both and all of us will have my last name. You'll be Sebastian and Charlie Stratford. Does that sound okay?"

"Can we keep our middle names?" Charlie asked. "Mine is Theodore and I like it because it's short for Teddy and that's also Bear's middle name."

Peter couldn't help but laugh at how adorable the kid was. "Yep, you can keep your middle name. Charles Theodore Stratford. Sounds like a future president's name to me."

"Okay. Then I'm fine with it," Charlie said with a firm nod.

"Awesome," Peter said, still chuckling. "You too, buddy?"

"Yep," Sebastian said. "Mom is so in *looooove* with you. She'll be really happy."

"Okay, then, let's get to work on this huge secret. I'm going to need a lot of help and if we can pull it off, it's going to be awesome."

Leaning in, he began to detail the boys on how he was going to propose to their mother.

Chapter 27

Two weeks later, Carrie stood in her bedroom, folding Sebastian's collar as he grimaced. "I hate this shirt, Mom," he said, sticking his finger between the collar and his neck. "It feels weird. I want to wear a t-shirt."

"Not for Thanksgiving dinner," she said, giving him a glare that indicated the discussion would end there. "Go help your brother fold his collar like I folded yours, okay?"

Rolling his eyes, he sighed. "Fine."

"Hey, buddy, you giving your mom a hard time?" Peter asked, strolling into the room.

"She's making me wear this stupid shirt."

"You won the battle when she let you wear your new sneakers," Peter said, sitting on the bed and gazing at Sebastian's shoes. "She was dead set on loafers but compromised on new kicks. Now you can play soccer in Ashlyn's back yard. I'd cut Mom some slack."

Sebastian was silent for a moment before his lips curved into the adorable smile that made everything else melt away. "Thanks for the sneakers, Mom. I really like them."

"You're welcome. Go help your brother, please, and make sure he's wearing his new sneakers too. The old ones are gross and we're throwing them out next time the garbage man comes."

"Okay," Sebastian said, bolting from the room.

Lowering to the bed, she collapsed on her back, hair splaying across the pillow. "How am I already exhausted? It's barely one p.m. Help."

Chuckling, he slithered over her and leaned on his hand, tracing her face with his fingertip. "Scott and Chad have promised to play soccer with them after we eat so that will zap some of their energy."

"Thank god. When we get home, I'm crashing super-hard. I'll probably be in a food coma anyway."

"After we bang, right? You're crashing super-hard after we bang?"

Rolling her eyes, she covered his face, attempting to push him away. "I can't even fathom that right now. You'd have to do something *really* special to get my lady juices flowing after I clean up Ashlyn's kitchen and treat myself with several glasses of wine afterward. But, if you can overcome those obstacles, maybe," she said, wrinkling her nose.

"Challenge accepted," he said, waggling his brows. "Something really special. I'll try my best."

Her eyes narrowed. "What's that look for? Your face is weird."

"Wow, thanks. You've got a way with compliments there, honey."

"Whatever. Your face did a funny thing for a second. Anyway, we should probably finish getting ready. I told Ashlyn I'd help her prepare the serving dishes."

"And Mark and I are going to look over the final contracts before we eat."

"I still can't believe Larry called and begged you to reconsider the Scranton opportunity. You must've really made an impression. I'm so proud of you."

"Definitely a shocker but he knows I'm serious about only managing that location. I've agreed to lay out a framework that's easily duplicatable at the Napa course and any others he wants to build. He'll get my suggestions on those sites and I've agreed to work remotely with anyone he hires. I think it's a win-win."

"And the firm is happy they're getting seven percent, although I think you could've talked them down to five."

Chuckling, he shook his head. "Man, you're a shark. I should've whisked you into the city and trained you to be a broker years ago. No one stands a chance against the stern mommy tone."

She arched a brow. "I would've only given you three percent so it would've been a waste of your time."

"I would've negotiated several *exams* from Nurse Longwood. That's the only payment I ever need."

She stared into his deep blue eyes, still amazed how free they were of any reservation or hesitation. He'd committed to her on every level and her heart swelled as it softly pounded.

"I can't believe it worked out so perfectly," she said, caressing his jaw. "We've had a pretty fortunate run here lately. Part of me wants to be scared it's too good to be true."

"Well, we had a pretty crappy run for multiple decades, so I think we might have earned it."

"We might have," she said, tears welling in her eyes. "I love you so much, Peter."

"I love you," he whispered, capturing her lips and sliding his tongue over hers as she wrapped her arms around his broad shoulders. Uttering a sexy growl, he shifted over her, jutting his erection into her thigh as she moaned.

"Okay," she said, gently pushing him away. "The door is open and we don't want to spur the 'how babies are made' talk today. There's too much do to."

"I can fit it in," he murmured, feathering light kisses across her neck.

Tugging his hair, she drew his head back. "Stop that right now, Peter Stratford. We have to go!"

"There it is," he said, nipping her lips. "You can't expect me to stop kissing you when you use the mommy tone, honey."

"You're incorrigible," she said before rolling out from under him. Standing she smoothed her hair. "Good grief, Peter."

"You look so beautiful with your hair mussed like that," he said, sitting up and resting his palms on the bed.

"Now I have to style it again. I'd be mad if you didn't just say something sappy and cute. Get up and go make sure the boys are presentable. Go!" she said, shooing him from the room.

After doing her hair a second time, she loaded up her purse, then loaded up the SUV and they headed to Ashlyn and Scott's.

The house smelled fantastic as they walked in and she handed the green bean casserole she'd made to Scott.

"Thanks, Carrie. Should I put it in the oven to heat it up?"

"Yes, or you can put it on the grill outside. I made sure it was in a foil pan so you could just plop it on the grill or in the oven. I can take it out back if you like."

"No, I've got it," he said, tugging the dish away. "The oven's full, so I'll place it on the grill. Be right back."

"I'm happy to help," she said, following him.

"Hey, Carrie," Ashlyn said, grabbing her wrist and tugging. "I actually need you over here. Grant's got this weird yellow mucus stuff coming out of his nose and I need your mom advice."

"Oh, okay," she said, getting the strange impression they didn't want her to walk onto the back porch. "Let me have a look. Sometimes babies just have weird excretions. It's terrifying when it's your first but by the time you guys have your second, you won't take them to the doctor unless they've broken out in hives."

Laughing, Ashlyn nodded. "I hope so. I'm fine, actually, but Scott is a bit neurotic. It's super sweet and he gets really grumpy when I point it out. We all know how much I love grumpy Scott."

"We do," she said, grinning. "And it makes sense with all he went through," Carrie said, sympathy welling in her chest. "Let me see the little munchkin. There he is!" she cried, reaching down and tickling Grant's chest with her finger. "How you doing, buddy?"

He definitely had some fluid running from his nose and a fair amount of drool but it seemed fine to Carrie.

"The fluids are clear from what I can see. I think he's fine. Just keep using the nasal aspirator when you see it appear."

"That's the baby fluid sucker thing, right?" Peter asked behind them, lifting a finger. "See? I've got this parenting thing down."

"Yeah, you're a real expert," Carrie muttered as Sebastian approached.

"Can we dig for the treasure before we eat, Ashlyn?" he asked, gazing up at her.

Ashlyn glanced at Carrie. "It's up to you. They might get dirty."

Carrie sighed, realizing that was a foregone conclusion when they played soccer later anyway. "Go ahead but please try your best to keep the dirt off your clothes and shoes, okay?"

"Okay!" the boys called before running outside.

Carrie settled into the kitchen, helping Ashlyn as Peter and Mark finalized the paperwork for the Scranton site in the living room. Eventually, the food was ready and they all sat at the massive dining room table Scott had built earlier this year for just this occasion.

"Thank you all for coming to our first Ardor Creek family dinner," Scott said, standing at the head of the table and lifting his glass. "Ashlyn and I think of all of you as family and we know how precious that is. I also want to send our prayers and thoughts to the people who aren't here today, with the hope they know we love them, wherever they are."

Ashlyn squeezed his hand, tears welling in her eyes, as she smiled up at him.

"To our loved ones," Carrie said, lifting her glass as everyone toasted along with her.

"I'm pretty sure today is going to turn out to be one of the most memorable days of our lives and I'm really excited about it. But first, let's eat this amazing meal my wife prepared. I'm so thankful for her, and her cooking skills," he teased, winking at Ashlyn, "and still hope she never figures out she's way too good for me because I'm really damn lucky."

"I'm stuck with him now, guys," she said, pointing to the baby sleeping beside her in the carrier. "Whether I like it or not."

"Okay, okay," Scott said, shooting her a playful glare. "We love you all very much and are so thankful you're here. Dig in and don't be afraid to have seconds or ask for more wine. We have plenty."

"Affirmative on the wine," Carrie joked, lifting her finger.

Everyone saluted Scott and they dug in, devouring the delicious food. Carrie took note of everyone at the table, most of them friends she'd known her whole life. Chad and Britney, who'd stuck around way longer than Carrie had anticipated, Mark, who was solo, Terry and her husband, Brian, Scott, Ashlyn, Peter, and her boys. Filled with so much gratitude, she took stock of how fortunate she was.

After the meal ended, Carrie was stuffed and took a moment to recover in the comfortable seat before helping Ashlyn clean and put the leftovers away. Once the huge task was complete, she sat on the living room couch and sipped her wine, enjoying the quiet. Narrowing her eyes, she realized it was really quiet. The boys were playing soccer with Chad and Scott in the back yard but that usually resulted in cheers and squeals that could be heard inside the house. Curious, she stood and ran into Ashlyn in the hallway.

"You heading outside?" Ashlyn asked.

"Yeah," Carrie said. "I took a moment of silence in the living room but figured I should join everyone while the sun is still out."

"Perfect timing," she said, white teeth flashing. "I think they're waiting for you."

"Uh, okay," Carrie said. "You coming?"

"Yep," she said, picking up the monitor as they trailed through the kitchen. "He's asleep in the crib. How freaking cute is that?"

"So adorable," she said, staring at Grant sleeping on the small screen. "You're lucky to have a baby that sleeps so much."

"Don't I know it. Hope it never changes. Go on, I'll follow you."

Carrie pushed open the back door, walking onto the wooden porch and glancing at the yard. A white altar stood in the middle of the grass and she looked at Ashlyn. "Did Scott build an altar?"

"Yep," Ashlyn said, gesturing for her to walk down the porch stairs. "Let's go see it."

Setting her glass on the table beside the grill, Carrie headed down the stairs, wondering where everyone else was. Once she stepped into the yard, she looked to her left and saw everyone lined up behind the boys, who held two big pieces of posterboard in their hands.

Lifting her hand to her pounding heart, she whispered. "What the heck is this?"

"Hey, Care Bear," Peter said, walking in front of the boys. He now wore a sport coat over his collared shirt and was giving her that goofy grin.

"Peter...?"

"Come on," he said, waving his hand. "We won't bite. And don't be weirded out because Terry's going to take a hundred pictures."

"Got the camera ready to go!" Terry yelled, a few feet to the side of everyone else.

Tentatively placing one foot in front of the other, Carrie approached until she was in front of Peter. "What are you doing?" she whispered.

"Uh, I think it's pretty obvious by now, honey." Pulling something from his pocket, he lowered to one knee as she lifted her fingers to her lips. Unable to control the tears, they streamed down her cheeks as Peter beamed up at her.

"Carrie Longwood, you are the love of my life. I messed up so many times with you and was sure I'd blown every single chance to be exactly where we are right now. But, low and behold, you let me back in and I'm so grateful for the opportunity to finally love you in the way you truly deserve."

He opened the box and Carrie saw a gorgeous diamond ring surrounded by tiny emeralds that must've cost a small fortune. Shaking her head, she emitted a sob. "That's too much, Peter."

"No way, Carrie. It's just the very beginning of everything you deserve. Everything I can't wait to give you." Glancing over his shoulder at the boys, he nodded. "Go for it, guys."

They flipped their signs around, Sebastian holding one that said *Will You Marry* and Charlie holding one that said ~~Uncle Peter~~...*Our Dad?*

Breaking into something between a sob, a laugh, and a cry of disbelief, Carrie furiously nodded. "Yes, Peter. Of course, I'll marry you."

Everyone cheered as he stood and took her hand, sliding the ring over her left finger. Carrie gazed at it, overcome with its extravagance. "This must've cost a fortune," she said, sliding her other arm around his neck and pulling him in for a kiss. "I would've been fine with the Cracker Jack ring you proposed with when we were ten."

Laughing, he kissed her as whistles sounded in the background. "This one's a tad bit nicer," he said, resting his forehead against hers. "Our wedding bands are a lot simpler though."

"Wedding bands?"

Clearing his throat, Chad stepped forward. "As mayor of our awesome little town, I can perform the ceremony today if you'd like to move forward, Carrie. You'll still have to secure the license next week and have me sign it. Mark's agreed to help with that but I can perform the ceremony right now. It's up to you."

"You set this up?" she asked Peter, overwhelmed.

"Yep. Scott built the altar for us and I told him there was a fifty/fifty chance you'd be willing to go through with it," he said, gesturing with his head toward the structure that sat a few feet away. "But I still have to pay Scott even if you say 'no' so I'm hoping you'll make it worth my investment."

"Stop joking," she said, swatting his chest. "Are you serious? You want to do this here? *Now*?"

"Yes, honey. If you want to. What better time than when we're surrounded by everyone we love? It's a day for gratitude and I'm so grateful to be in your and the boys' lives."

Inhaling a deep breath, she observed her friends, expressions filled with love as they waited for her answer. Glancing at the boys, she asked, "What do you guys say? Do you want me to marry Peter today?"

"Yes!" they both exclaimed, jumping up and down.

"Do it, Mom!" Sebastian said, excited. "He loves you and you love him and that's how marriage works."

"Well, thank you for that sage advice," she said, laughing.

"Come on," Charlie said, grabbing her hand before Sebastian grabbed Peter's. They tugged them to the altar and Sebastian pointed at the ground. "You stand here, Mom, and Dad stands here and Chad stands here," he said, directing everyone. "They showed us while you were inside. I told Dad I'd help so it would be perfect."

"It's so perfect," she said, sliding her hand over his hair. "Where do you and Charlie stand?"

"Here!" they both called, falling into position.

"Well," Chad said, taking his proper spot and pulling some papers from his pocket. "Seems like this is happening. Please take each other's hands and we'll get this ceremony underway."

Placing her shaking hands in Peter's, she squeezed tight. "We're really doing this?"

"We're really doing this," he said, clenching her hands. He seemed so calm and sure as he stood before her, achingly handsome in the waning November sunlight. Feeling her chin tremble, Carrie tried to keep it together.

"Take a breath, Care Bear," he said, gently squeezing. "We were always going to end up here. It's our time. I love you."

"I love you," she whispered, inhaling the crisp air, shoulders softening as she settled into the moment. Staring into his eyes, she repeated Chad's words, vowing to honor and cherish him before Peter did the same.

Once the ceremony was finished, Chad stuffed the papers back into his coat and said, "Well, kiss the bride already, man!"

Peter pulled her into his arms, kissing her so sweetly as their loved ones cheered and clapped. Overwhelmed with emotion, she held him tight. "I can't believe this."

"Believe it, Mrs. Stratford. You're finally my wife. Holy shit."

"Woo hoo!" she exclaimed as everyone laughed. The boys threw their arms around their waists and Carrie hugged her family as disbelief still coursed through her veins.

Peter winked at her and waggled his brows. "Remember, we had a deal about what would happen if I did something really special. Don't forget."

Tossing back her head, she broke into joyful laughter. "Oh, yeah, that promise is definitely being kept. Can't wait."

"Me either."

There, on the soft grass under the rapidly dimming sky, the Stratford family celebrated their first official day, although the ceremony wasn't needed to prove what Carrie already knew in her heart: she and Peter had always been family. They'd just needed a few extra years to cement it. Clutching him close, she closed her eyes and sent a silent prayer of thanks to the universe, excited to begin their next chapter.

Chapter 28

I t took forever to get the boys to sleep that night which was understandable due to the day's events. Finally, Carrie trailed into the bedroom at nearly eleven o'clock, locking the door behind her, and heard Peter brushing his teeth.

"Did Charlie finally go to sleep?" he asked from the adjoining bathroom.

"Yes," she said, kicking off her slippers and sliding off the sweatpants she'd changed into when they got home. "He says he finally saw the ghost leave his room and he's okay to sleep in there now. I love him dearly but there was no way he was sleeping in here tonight."

Tugging her sweatshirt over her head, she rummaged in her drawer for one of the tank tops she usually slept in.

"Excuse me, Mrs. Stratford," he said, appearing at her side and grasping her wrist. "Are you putting on clothes to come to bed? We had a deal."

Turning, she slid her arms around his neck and grinned. "Did we? I can't seem to remember..."

Yelping, she clutched his shoulders for dear life as he bent down and lifted her in one fell swoop. Carrying her to the bed, he tossed her on top before crawling over her.

"You bring out these caveman vibes in me, Carrie," he said, giving her a wet kiss as he loomed over her. "God, you're so sexy. I'm the luckiest man in the fucking world."

"Well," she said, sliding her arms over her head and resting them there as he stared at her with lust-filled eyes. "Ravish me then, Mr. Caveman. That sounds fun." She chucked her eyebrows.

Giving a measured grunt, he balanced on his knees, straddling her. Sliding his hands underneath, he unclasped her bra and tore it from her body. Biting her lip, Carrie felt her nipples pucker in the cool air.

"Leave your hands above your head," he commanded, lowering to kiss her before sucking her bottom lip between his teeth.

"Yes, sir," was her sultry reply.

Trailing a string of kisses over her neck and across her chest, he came to her breast and nudged it. "Your nipples always get so fucking hard when we make love, Carrie," he said, licking the taut nub. "It's so hot."

"Peter..."

Opening his mouth, he sucked her deep, tugging her breast between his lips, creating such decadent pleasure. Sparks of desire flashed through her body as slickness coated her core. Rubbing her thighs together, she pushed her flesh into his mouth, wanting more. Wanting everything he could give her.

"You little tease," he said, releasing her breast from his mouth only to slide his hand over it and squeeze. Kissing a trail to her other breast, he devoured it as he twisted her wet nipple between his fingers. "You like to tease me with these tight little nipples, don't you, honey?"

"Yes," she cried, closing her lids against the immense pleasure. "Sometimes you walk into the office and you look so good. My nipples are so hard when you're talking to me."

"Goddammit," he cursed, rising and capturing her mouth in a torrid kiss as he squeezed her nipple. "You know I'll never be able to look at you in the office again without thinking about that, right?"

Raking her teeth over her lip, she nodded. "Mmm-hmm..."

Breathing a ragged laugh, he gave her another sloppy kiss. "I'm going to fuck you hard for those dirty thoughts, honey."

"Good," she said, pushing his head back to her breast. "Get on with it."

"Still a little witch in the bedroom," he said, chuckling as he nipped both of her breasts before continuing to trail kisses down her abdomen. Sticking his tongue in her navel, she squirmed before he moved lower. Settling on his knees beside the bed, he gripped her hips and dragged her to the edge. Lifting her legs over his shoulders, he clutched her lacy panties and ripped them off.

"I'm not going to have any underwear left if you keep doing that."

"Quiet, woman," he said, blue eyes darkened with desire as he stared at her from between her legs. "Open that sweet pussy for me." Placing his palms on her inner thighs, he pushed her open and buried his face between her legs.

"Oh, god, Peter," she cried, thrusting her fingers in his hair as he flicked his tongue along her swollen folds. "Oh, fuck! It's too much."

He groaned against her, the vibrating sound only adding to the pleasure as he circled his tongue over her wet skin before impaling her drenched opening. Gaze locked with hers, he plunged his tongue deep inside, withdrawing before surging in once again. Lost in the intimate moment, she drew him closer, tugging his hair as he moaned. Gliding his hand to her clit, he began stimulating the tiny nub as he fucked her with his tongue, the motions furious as her body quivered on the bed.

"*Peter...I can't take it...it's so much...*"

"Yes, you can," he murmured, increasing the maddening rubbing of his fingers on her clit. "Come on my face, Carrie. I want you all over my tongue. Do you hear me?"

Whimpering, she pushed into his fingers, losing all control when he jutted his tongue inside her once again. Tossing her head back on the bed, she exploded, screaming his name as the orgasm took hold, wracking her body with tremor upon tremor until she thought her muscles might disintegrate.

High-pitched mewls surrounded them as she experienced one of the most encompassing orgasms of her life. Unable to process anything but the intense pleasure, her arms flailed before finding the comforter and clenching it in a death grip as she convulsed.

Before the trembling abated, he crawled over her and lifted her leg, aligning his body with hers.

"Don't stop coming," he said, running his shaft through her slick essence. "Keep coming while I fuck you, honey." Gazing into her soul, he impaled her with one swift stroke, gritting his teeth as his body tensed.

She whimpered, her ravaged body accepting the invasion as she gripped his shoulders.

"You okay?" he asked, undulating into her as he held her leg high.

"Yes. Harder!" she cried, opening her body to him.

"Is this what you want?" he gritted, slamming his hips against her as he groaned. "God, you feel amazing. I'm going to fuck you like this forever."

Throwing back her head, she laughed as his balls slapped against her, the sounds of their colliding flesh so erotic as they reverberated off the walls. "That's impossible—"

"I don't care," he said, burying his face in her neck as he groaned. "Oh, *fuck*...am I hitting it, honey? I want to take you there again."

"Yes!" she cried, the sizzling bundle of nerves pulsing each time he jutted against it with the head of his cock. "Right there. Don't stop. Oh, god, Peter...I'm going to come again...please...*fuck!*

Her body snapped as the bundle of nerves went into overdrive, shooting tiny sparks of endless joy to every cell in her body. Carrie lost all semblance of time and space as her lover maneuvered inside her deepest place, reaching for his own release. Clutching him tight, she struggled to breathe as the climax took over, rendering her brain all but useless.

He groaned her name into the slippery skin of her neck before his muscles tensed as his hips began to buck furiously. Murmuring unintelligible words of love and desire, she held him close as he emptied himself into her, wondering if this would be the night they added to their family. Since her IUD had been removed, anything was possible, although she wasn't sure how easily she could conceive now that she'd reached forty. Longing began to take hold as she imagined a baby with Peter's cute little dimple and she hugged him close, feeling him pulse inside her.

He murmured her name as his body jerked, dispersing the final jets of release. Wrapping her legs around his back, she crossed her ankles, embracing him in every way possible.

"I love when you wrap around me like that, honey," he said, kissing her neck. "You always push into me when we make love. It's so fucking sweet."

"I've always wanted to be close to you. Even when you got that terrible mohawk haircut in eighth grade."

Lifting his head, he brushed a tuft of hair off her forehead as he snickered. "You're lucky I didn't grow a mullet. I was this close." He held his thumb and forefinger a centimeter apart.

"That would've definitely been the end of our relationship. Thank goodness you restrained yourself."

"You still would've been mad for me. Come on, woman."

"Not likely," she teased, stroking his cheek. "You really outdid yourself today, Mr. Stratford. Wow. Eighteen-year-old Carrie could've never imagined what you did in her wildest dreams."

"Well, I hope forty-year-old Carrie Elizabeth Longwood Stratford feels it was worth the wait. The road was pretty shitty, and I'm really sorry for that, but today was pretty freaking awesome."

"Today was the best day of my life, along with when I had Sebastian and Charlie. Thank you, Peter. You made me feel so special."

"I love you so much, Carrie," he said, pecking her lips. "There's so much more you deserve. I can't wait to give it to you."

"I know," she said, incapable of stopping the tear that slid down her cheek, shivering when he kissed it away.

"In the meantime, we need to buy you more cute little panties because I'm really digging the whole 'rip them off your body' thing."

Laughing, she sifted her fingers through his hair. "I'm really digging it too."

Sated and content, they discussed other silly things they wanted to incorporate into their sexy times before Carrie yawned.

"Okay, sleeping beauty. I think we need to clean up and call it a night. This was a long day." Slowly rising, he extended his hand and led her to the bathroom.

Once they were in bed, he spooned her close and rested his lips against the shell of her ear.

"Goodnight, Carrie Elizabeth Stratford."

Chuckling, she wiggled her butt into him. "Goodnight, Peter. Thank you for making my high school doodling dreams a reality."

His soft laughter tickled her neck until her eyes began to droop and she relaxed in his arms. Giving in to the darkness, she fell asleep, surrounded by the peaceful cadence of her husband's deep breaths.

Epilogue

♥

Two years later...

Carrie buzzed around the house, sliding the earring through her ear as she hopped on one foot and tugged on her heel.

"Peter!" she called, trying to remember where the box was that held the clutches she'd packed. "Did we put the extra bedroom boxes in the garage or the den?"

"Den!" he yelled from the upstairs bedroom as Emily wailed at the top of her lungs.

Striding through the door, she found the box located in the den of their new five-bedroom home and located the clutch she wanted to bring. Heading to the living room, she found Charlie rocking the bassinet as his sister wailed inside.

"Sorry, Mom," he said, looking as frazzled as she felt. "I tried to rock her but she won't stop crying."

"You're such a good big brother," Carrie said, kissing his thick hair. "Sometimes, babies just cry for no reason." Reaching down, she lifted Emily and held her to her chest, softly patting her back. "Okay, sweetie, Mommy's here. Shhh..."

Her daughter continued to cry as Sebastian burst into the room. "We're going to be late, Mom! I have to make sure the ring is tied really tight to Kitana so I can walk her down the aisle."

"Yes, I know you've been designated as the Supervisor to the Ring Bearer," she said, reaching down and smoothing his hair. "It's an important job Chad felt only you could do. Thankfully, Kitana is a dog and won't mind if we're a few minutes late."

"Why is everyone screaming?" Peter teased, breezing into the room. "Here, honey, let me hold her," he said, extending his arms. Carrie handed over their daughter, who ceased crying immediately as she gazed at Peter while he spoke tender baby talk to her.

"That's my sweet girl," he cooed, kissing her forehead. "No crying today. It's a happy day." Lifting his gaze to Carrie, he grinned. "What?"

"I'd be annoyed she always stops crying when you hold her but it's also pretty helpful in situations like this." Lifting to her toes, she kissed his temple and whispered, "I'll let you live. This time."

"Still rocking the serial killer vibes," he said, scrunching his features. "Are we stuck in some weird Lifetime movie where you're the stalker and I'm the devilishly handsome male lead?"

"Not in million years," she said, rolling her eyes. "Okay, boys, let's hop in the car," she said, pointing to the front door. "Sebastian, please sit in the last row so your brother can sit beside Emily in the car seat."

"Okay!" he called as they sped out the door.

Expelling a breath, she smiled at her husband. "Well, I'm sure we've forgotten a hundred things, but let's get on the road. I'll grab her diaper bag."

"Hey," Peter said, encircling her wrist and drawing her close. "Hang with me for one sec and look at this amazing human we created." Emily's cheek rested on his chest as she sucked her fist between her tiny lips. "She has the same three freckles you have on her nose right there," he said, pointing.

"And she has your dimple," Carrie said, sliding her arm around his waist and resting her head on his shoulder. "She's kind of perfect."

"Yeah," he said, swaying as Emily's eyelids drooped. "Can't wait to tell her she can finally date...when she's thirty-five."

Snickering, Carrie slapped his pec. "Careful not to make the same mistakes Pastor Longwood made. He pushed me right into your forbidden arms."

Peter scowled. "Damn. I need to rethink this whole dad thing. Give me a minute."

"Can't even give you a second. We're late as it is. Chad's finally tying the knot. Holy crap! Come on." Extending her hand, she waited.

Peter slid his palm over hers, lacing their fingers as he held their daughter. Grabbing the carrier, Carrie led them outside, excited to see the most eligible bachelor in Ardor Creek marry the love of his life.

Before You Go

W ell, did you adore Carrie and Peter as much as I did? I hope so! I *really* enjoyed writing their story and their heartfelt attempts to finally get it right. Looks like Chad Hanson, Ardor Creek mayor and player extraordinaire is getting married at some point in the future...but I have one more story to tell first. Remember Scott's therapist, Dr. Teresa Roe, from Hearts Reclaimed? Well, she ends up meeting sexy attorney Mark Lancaster and sparks fly! You can read their book, **Desires Uncovered**, right now! Thanks so much for spending some time in Ardor Creek with me!

P lease consider leaving a review on your retailer's site, Book-Bub, and/or Goodreads. Your reviews help spread the word for indie authors so we can keep writing smokin' hot books for you to devour. Thanks so much for reading!

About the Author

Ayla Asher is the pen name for a USA Today bestselling author who writes steamy fantasy romance under a different pseudonym. However, she loves a spicy, fast-paced contemporary romance too! Therefore, she's decided to share some of her contemporary stories, hoping to spread a little joy one HEA at a time. She would love to connect with you on social media, where she enjoys making dorky TikToks, FB/IG posts and fun book trailers!

ALSO BY AYLA ASHER

<u>Manhattan Holiday Loves Trilogy</u>
Book 1: His Holiday Pact
Book 2: Her Valentine Surprise
Book 3: Her Patriotic Prince

<u>Ardor Creek Series</u>
Book 1: Hearts Reclaimed
Book 2: Illusions Unveiled
Book 3: Desires Uncovered
Book 4: Resolutions Embraced
Book 5: Passions Fulfilled
Book 6: Futures Entwined

www.ingramcontent.com/pod-product-compliance
Lightning Source LLC
Chambersburg PA
CBHW070941190726
48292CB00004B/1293